FROM THE LAND OF THE SNOW-PEARLS

FROM THE LAND OF THE SNOW-PEARLS

TALES FROM PUGET SOUND

By ELLA HIGGINSON.

Short Story Index Reprint Series

BOOKS FOR LIBRARIES PRESS
FREEPORT, NEW YORK

First Published 1897
Reprinted 1970

STANDARD BOOK NUMBER:
8369-3553-5

LIBRARY OF CONGRESS CATALOG CARD NUMBER:
70-122720

PRINTED IN THE UNITED STATES OF AMERICA

TO

RUSSELL CARDEN HIGGINSON

Puget Sound lies in its emerald setting like a great blue sapphire, which at sunset, draws to its breast all the marvelous and splendid coloring of the fire-opal. Around it, shining through their rose-colored mists like pearls upon the soft blue or green of the sky, are linked the great snow-mountains, so beautiful and so dear, that those who love this land with a proud and passionate love, have come to think of it, fondly and poetically, as "the land of the snow-pearls."

CONTENTS

THE FLOWER THAT GREW IN THE SAND

THE FLOWER THAT GREW IN THE SAND

Demaris opened the gate and walked up the narrow path. There was a low hedge of pink and purple candytuft on each side. Inside the hedges were little beds of homely flowers in the shapes of hearts, diamonds and Maltese crosses.

Mrs. Eaton was stooping over a rosebush, but she arose when she heard the click of the gate. She stood looking at Demaris, with her arms hanging stiffly at her sides.

"Oh," she said, with a grim smile; "you, is it?"

"Yes," said the girl, blushing and looking embarrassed. "Ain't it a nice evenin'?"

"It is that; awful nice. I'm tyin' up my rose-bushes. Won't you come in an' set down a while?"

"Oh, my, no!" said Demaris. Her eyes went wistfully to the pink rosebush. "I can't stay."

"Come fer kindlin' wood?"

"No." She laughed a little at the worn-out

joke. "I come to see 'f you had two or three pink roses to spare."

"Why, to be sure, a dozen if you want. Just come an' help yourself. My hands ain't fit to tech 'em after diggin' so."

She stood watching the girl while she carefully selected some half-open roses. There was a look of good-natured curiosity on her face.

"Anything goin' on at the church to-night?"

"No; at least not that I know of."

"It must be a party then."

"No—not a party, either." She laughed merrily. Her face was hidden as she bent over the roses, but her ears were pink under the heavy brown hair that fell, curling, over them.

"Well, then, somebody's comin' to see you."

"No; I'll have to tell you." She lifted a glad, shy face. "I'm goin' on the moonlight excursion."

"Oh, now! Sure? Well, I'm reel glad."

"So'm I. I never wanted to go anywheres so much in my life. I've been 'most holdin' my breath for fear ma'd get sick."

"How is your ma?"

"Well, she ain't very well; she never is, you know."

"What ails her?"

"I do' know," said Demaris, slowly. "We'll get home by midnight. So 'f she has a spell

2

come on, pa can set up with her till I get home, and then I can till mornin'."

"Should think you'd be all wore out a-settin' up two or three nights a week that way."

Demaris sighed. The radiance had gone out of her face and a look of care was upon it.

"Well," she said, after a moment, "I'll have a good time to-night, anyhow. We're goin' to have the band along. They're gettin' so's they play reel well. They play 'Annie Laurie' an' 'Rocked 'n the Cradle o' the Deep,' now."

The gate clicked. A child came running up the path.

"Oh, sister, sister! Come home quick!"

"What for?" said Demaris. There was a look of dread on her face.

"Ma's goin' right into a spell. She wants you quick. She thinks she's took worse 'n usual."

There was a second's hesitation. The girl's face whitened. Her lips trembled.

"I guess I won't want the roses after gettin' 'em," she said. "I'm just as much obliged, though, Mis' Eaton."

She followed the child to the gate.

"Well, if that don't beat all!" ejaculated Mrs. Eaton, looking after her with genuine sympathy. "It just seems as if she had a spell to order ev'ry time that girl wants to go anywheres. It's nothin' but hysterics, anyway. I'd like to doctor her for a while. I'd souze a bucket o' cold water over her! I reckon that 'u'd fetch her to 'n a hurry.''

She laughed with a kind of stern mirth and resumed her work.

Demaris hurried home. The child ran at her side. Once she took her hand and gave her an upward look of sympathy.

She passed through the kitchen, laying her roses on the table. Then she went into her mother's room.

Mrs. Ferguson lay on a couch. A white cloth was banded around her head, coming well down over one eye. She was moaning bitterly.

Demaris looked at her without speaking.

"Where on earth you been?" She gave the girl a look of fierce reproach. "A body might die, fer all the help you'd be to 'em. Here I've been a-feelin' a spell a-comin' on all day, an' yet you go a-gaddin' 'round to the neighbors, leavin' me to get along the best way I know how. I believe this is my last spell. I've got that awful pain over my right eye ag'in, till I'm nearly crazy. My liver's all out o' order."

Demaris was silent. When one has heard the cry of "wolf" a hundred times, one is inclined to be incredulous. Her apathetic look angered her mother.

"What makes you stand there a-starin' like a

4

dunce? Can't you help a body? Get the camfire bottle an' the tincture lobelia an' the box o' goose grease! You know's well's me what I need when I git a spell. I'm so nervous I feel's if I c'u'd fly. I got a horrible feelin' that this'll be my last spell—an' yet you stand there a-starin' 's if you didn't care a particle!"

Demaris moved about the room stiffly, as if every muscle in her body were in rebellion. She took from a closet filled with drugs the big camphor bottle with its cutglass stopper, the little bottle labeled "tinc. lobelia," and the box of goose grease.

She placed a chair at the side of the couch to hold the bottle. "Oh, take that old split-bottom cheer away!" exclaimed her mother. "Everything upsets on it so! Get one from the kitchen—the one that's got cherries painted on the back of it. What makes you ac' so? You know what cheer I want. You'd tantalize the soul out of a saint!"

The chair was brought. The bottles were placed upon it. Demaris stood waiting.

"Now rub my head with the camfire, or I'll go ravin' crazy. I can't think where 't comes from!"

The child stood twitching her thin fingers around a chair. She watched her mother in a matter-of-course way. Demaris leaned over the couch in an uncomfortable position and cómmenced the slow, gentle massage that must continue all night. She did not lift her eyes. They were full of tears.

For a long time there was silence in the room. Mrs. Ferguson lay with closed eyes. Her face wore a look of mingled injury and reproach.

"Nellie," said Demaris, after a while, "could you make a fire in the kitchen stove? Or would you rather try to do this while I build it?"

"Hunh-unh," said the child, shaking her head with emphasis. "I'd ruther build fires any time."

"All right. Put two dippers 'o water 'n the tea-kettle. Be sure you get your dampers right. An' I guess you might wash some potatoes an' put 'em in to bake. They'll be done by time pa comes, an' he can stay with ma while I warm up the rest o' the things. Ma, what could you eat?"

"Oh, I do' know"—in a slightly mollified tone. "A piece o' toast, mebbe—'f you don't get it too all-fired hard."

"Well, I'll try not."

Nellie went out, and there was silence in the room. The wind came in through the open window, shaking little ripples of perfume into the room. The sun was setting and a broad band of reddish gold sunk down the wall.

Demaris watched it sinking lower, and thought how slowly the sun was settling behind the

6

straight pines on the crests of the blue mountains.

"Oh," said Mrs. Ferguson, "what a wretched creature I am! Just a-sufferin' day an' night, year in an' year out, an' a burden on them that I've slaved fer all my life. Many's the night I've walked with you 'n my arms till mornin', Demaris, an' never knowed what it was to git sleepy or tired. An' now you git mad the minute I go into a spell."

Demaris stood upright with a tortured look.

"Oh, ma," she exclaimed. Her voice was harsh with pain. "I ain't mad. Don't think I'm mad. I can't cry out o' pity ev'ry time you have a spell, or I'd be cryin' all the time. An' besides, to-night I'm so—disappointed."

"What you disappointed about?"

"Why, you know." Her lips trembled. "The excursion."

Mrs. Ferguson opened her eyes.

"Oh, I'd clean fergot that."

She looked as if she were thinking she would really have postponed the spell, if she had remembered. "That's too bad, Demaris. That's always the way." She began to cry helplessly. "I'm always in the way. Always mis'rable myself, an' always makin' somebody else mis'rable. I don't see what I was born fer."

"Never you mind." Demaris leaned over suddenly and put her arms around her mother. "Don't you think I'm mad. I'm just disap-

7

pointed. Now don't cry. You'll go and make yourself worse. An' there comes pa; I hear him cleanin' his boots on the scraper.''

Mr. Ferguson stumbled as he came up the steps to the kitchen. He was very tired. He was not more than fifty, but his thin frame had a pitiable stoop. The look of one who has struggled long and failed was on his brown and wrinkled face. His hair and beard were prematurely gray. His dim blue eyes had a hopeless expression that was almost hidden by a deeper one of patience. He wore a coarse flannel shirt, moist with perspiration, and faded blue overalls. His boots were wrinkled and hard; the soil of the fields clung to them. " Sick ag'in, ma?" he said.

"Sick ag'in! Mis'rable creature that I am! I've got that awful pain over my right eye ag'in. I can't think where it comes from. I'm nearly crazy with it.''

"Well, I guess you'll feel a little better after you git some tea. I'll go an' wash, an' then rub your head, while Demaris gits a bite to eat. I've plowed ever since sun-up, an' I'm tired an' hungry.''

He returned in a few minutes, and took Demaris's place. He sighed deeply, but silently, as he sat down.

Demaris set the table and spread upon it the simple meal which she had prepared. "I'll stay with ma while you an' pa eat," said Nellie, with a sudden burst of unselfishness.

"Well," said Demaris, wearily.

Mr. Ferguson sat down at the table and leaned his head on his hand. "I'm too tired to eat," he said; "hungry's I am." He looked at the untempting meal of cold boiled meat, baked potatoes and apple sauce.

Demaris did not lift her eyes as she sat down. She felt that she ought to say something cheerful, but her heart was too full of her own disappointment. She despised her selfishness even while yielding to it.

"It does beat all about your ma," said her father. "I can't see where she gits that pain from. It ain't nothin' danger's or it 'u'd a-killed her long ago. It almost seems 's if she jests gits tired o' bein' well, an' begins to git scared fer fear that pain's a-comin' on—an' then it comes right on. I've heard her say lots o' times that she'd been well a whole week now, but that she w'u'dn't brag or that pain 'u'd come on—an' inside of an hour it 'ud up an' come on. It's awful discouragin'."

"I wish I was dead!" said Demaris.

Her father did not speak. His silence reproached her more than any words could have done.

9

When she went into the bedroom again she
found her mother crying childishly.

"Demaris, did I hear you say you wished you
was dead?"

"I guess so.   I said it."

"Well, God Almighty knows I wish I was!
You don't stop to think what 'u'd become o' me
'f it wa'n't fer you.   Your pa c'u'dn't hire anybody, an' he's gittin' too old to set up o' nights
after workin' hard all day.   You'd like to see 't
all come on your little sister, I reckon."

Demaris thought of those slim, weak wrists,
and shivered.   Her mother commenced to sob—
and that aggravated the pain.

Demaris stooped and put her arms around her
and kissed her.

"I'm sorry I said it," she whispered.   "I didn't
mean it.   I'm just tired an' cross.   You know I
didn't mean it."

Her father came in heavily.

"Demaris," he said, "Frank Vickers is comin'
'round to the front door.   I'll take keer o' your
ma while you go in an' see him."

It was a radiant-faced young fellow that walked
into Demaris's little parlor.   He took her hand
with a tenderness that brought the color beating
into her cheeks.

"What?" he said.   "An' you ain't ready?
Why, the boat leaves in an hour, an' it's a good,

long walk to the wharf. You'll have to hurry up, Demaris.''

''I can't go.''

''You can't go? Why can't you?''

She lifted her eyes bravely. Then tears swelled into them very slowly until they were full. Not one fell. She looked at him through them. He felt her hand trembling against the palm of his own.

''Why can't you, Demaris?''

''My mother's sick—just hear her moanin' clear in here.''

Young Vickers's face was a study.

''Why, she was sick last time I wanted to take you som'ers—to a dance, wasn't it?''

''Yes—I know.''

''An' time before that, when I wanted you to go to a church sociable up'n String Town.''

''Yes.''

''Why, she must be sick near onto all the time, accordin' to that.''

''She is—pretty near.'' She withdrew her hand. There was a stiff-looking lounge in one corner of the room. It was covered with Brussels carpet, and had an uncomfortable back, but it was dear to Demaris's heart. She had gathered and sold strawberries two whole summers to pay for it. She sat down on it now and laid her hands together on her knees.

The young man followed and sat down beside her.

"Why, my dear," he said, very quietly, "you can't stand this sort of thing—it's wearin' you out. You never did look light an' happy like other girls o' your age; an' lately you're gettin' a real pinched look. I feel as if 't was time for me to interfere." He took her hand again.

It was dim twilight in the room now. Demaris turned her head aside. The tears brimmed over and fell fast and silently.

"Interferin' won't do no good," she said, resolutely. "There's just two things about it. My mother's sick all the time, an' I have to wait on her. There's nobody else to do it."

"Well, as long 's you stay at home it'll all come on you. You ain't able to carry sech a load."

"I'll have to."

"Demaris, you'll just have to leave."

"What!" said the girl. She turned to look at him in a startled way. "Leave home? I couldn't think of doin' that."

He leaned toward her and put his arm around her, trembling strongly. "Not even to come to my home, Demaris? I want you, dear; an' I won't let you kill yourself workin', either. I ain't rich, but I'm well enough off to give you a comfortable home an' some one to do your work for you."

There was a deep silence. Each felt the full beating of the other's heart. There was a rose-bush under the window, an old-fashioned one. Its blooms were not beautiful, but they were very sweet. It had flung a slim, white spray of them into the room. Demaris never smelled their fragrance afterward without a keen, exquisite thrill of passion, as brief as it was delicious.

"I can't, Frank." Her tone was low and uncertain. "I can't leave my mother. She's sick an' gettin' old. I can't."

"Oh, Demaris! That's rank foolishness!"

"Well, I guess it's the right kind of foolishness." She drew away and sat looking at him. Her hands were pressed together in her lap.

"Why, it ain't expected that a girl 'ad ought to stay an' take care o' her mother forever, is it? It ain't expected that she ought to turn herself into a hospital nurse, is it?"

Her face grew stern.

"Don't talk that way, Frank. That ain't respectful to my mother. She's had a hard life an' so's my father. You know I want to come, but I can't. It's my place to stay an' take care o' her. I'm goin' to do it—hard 's it is. My leavin' 'em 'u'd just take the heart out of both of 'em. An' there's Nellie, too."

"Demaris—" he spoke slowly; his face was pale—"I'm goin' to say somethin' to you I never thought I'd say to any girl alive. But the fact is, I didn't know till right now how much I think o' you. You marry me, an' we'll all live together?"

Her face softened. She leaned a little toward him with uncontrollable tenderness. But as he made a quick movement, she drew back.

"No, Frank. I can't—I can't! It won't do. Such things is what breaks women's hearts!"

"What things, dear?"

"Folks livin' together that way. There's no good ever comes of it. I'd have to set up with mother just the same, an' you'd be worryin' all the time for fear it 'u'd make me sick, an' you'd be wantin' to set up with 'er yourself."

"Of course," he said, stoutly. "I'd expect to. That's what I mean. I'd take some o' your load off o' you."

Demaris smiled mournfully. "You don't know what it is, Frank. It's all very well to talk about it, but when it comes to doin' it you'd be tired out 'n a month. You'd wish you hadn't married me—an' that 'u'd kill me!"

"I wouldn't. Oh, Demaris, just you try me. I'll be good to all your folks—just as good's can be, dear. I swear it."

She leaned toward him again with a sob. He took her in his arms. He felt the delicious

14

warmth of her body. Their lips trembled together.

After a while she drew away slowly and looked
at him earnestly in the faint light.

"If I thought you wouldn't change," she faltered. "I know you mean it now, but oh—"

"Sister," called a thin, troubled voice from the
hall; "can't you come here just a minute?"

Demaris went at once, closing the door behind
her.

The child threw her slim arms around her
sister's waist, sobbing.

"Oh, sister, I forgot to get the kindlin' wood,
an' now it's so dark down cellar. I'm afraid.
Can't you come with me?"

"Wait a few minutes, dear, an' I will. Frank
won't stay long to-night."

"Oh, won't he? I'm so glad." Her voice
sunk to a whisper. "I hate to have him here,
sister. He takes you away from us so much, an'
ev'rything goes wrong when you ain't here. Ma's
offul bad to-night, an' pa looks so tired! Don't
let him stay long, sister. He don't need you as
bad 's we do."

She tiptoed into the kitchen. Demaris stood
still in the hall. The moon was coming, large
and silver, over the hill. Its soft light brought
her slender figure out of the dark, and set a halo
above her head bending on its fair neck, like a

flower on its stem. Her lips moved, but the prayer remained voiceless in her heart.

A moan came from her mother's room.

"Oh, paw, you hurt my head! Your hand 's terrable rough! Is that girl goin' to stay in there forever?"

Demaris lifted her head and walked steadily into the poor little parlor. "I'll have to ask you to go now, Frank; my mother needs me."

"Well, dear." He reached his strong young arms to her. She stood back, moving her head from side to side.

"No, Frank. I can't marry you, now or ever. My mother comes first."

"But you ain't taken time to make up your mind, Demaris. I'll wait fer 'n answer."

"It's no use. I made up my mind out 'n the hall. You might as well go. When I make up my mind it's no use in tryin' to get me to change it. I hadn't made it up before."

He went to her and took her hands.

"Demaris," he said, and all his heart-break was in his voice, "do you mean it? Oh, my dear, I'll go if you send me; but I'll never come back again; never."

She hesitated but a second. Then she said very gently, without emotion—"Yes, go. You've been good to me; but it's all over. Good-bye."

He dropped her hands without a word, and went.

She did not look after him, or listen to his foot-steps. She went to the cellar with Nellie, to get the kindling wood, which she arranged in the stove, ready for the match in the morning.

Then she went into her mother's room. She looked pale in the flickering light of the candle.

"I'll take care of ma, now, pa," she said. "You get to bed an' rest. I know you're all tired out—plowin' ever since sun-up! An' don't you get up till I call you. I ain't a bit sleepy. I couldn't sleep if I went to bed."

She moistened her fingers with camphor and commenced bathing her mother's brow.

ESTHER'S "FOURTH"

ESTHER'S "FOURTH"

It was the fourth day of July, and the fourth hour of the day. Long, beryl ribbons of color were streaming through the lovely Grand Ronde valley when the little girl awoke—so suddenly and so completely that it seemed as if she had not been asleep at all.

"Sister!" she cried in a thin, eager voice. "Ain't it time to get up? It's just struck four."

"Not yet," said the older girl drowsily. "There's lots o' time, Pet."

She put one arm under the child affectionately and fell asleep again. The little girl lay motionless, waiting. There was a large cherry tree outside, close to the tiny window above her bed, and she could hear the soft turning of the leaves, one against the other, and the fluttering of the robins that were already stealing the cherries. Innocent thieves that they were, they continually betrayed themselves by their shrill cries of triumph.

Not far from the tiny log-cabin the river went singing by on its way through the green valley; hearing it, Esther thought of the soft glooms under the noble balm trees, where the grouse

21

drummed and butterflies drifted in long level flight. Esther always breathed softly while she watched the butterflies—she had a kind of reverence for them—and she thought there could be nothing sweeter, even in heaven, than the scents that the wind shook out of the balms.

She lay patiently waiting with wide eyes until the round clock in the kitchen told her that another hour had gone by. "Sister," she said then, "oh, it must be time to get up! I just *can't* wait any longer."

The older girl, with a sleepy but sympathetic smile, slipped out of bed and commenced dressing. The child sprang after her. "Sister," she cried, running to the splint-bottomed chair on which lay the cheap but exquisitely white undergarments. "I can't hardly wait. Ain't it good of Mr. Hoover to take me to town? Oh, I feel as if I had hearts all over me, an' every one of 'em beating so!"

"Don't be so excited, Pet." The older sister smiled gently at the child. "Things never are quite as nice as you expect them to be," she added, with that wisdom that comes so soon to starved country hearts.

"Well, this can't help bein' nice," said the child, with a beautiful faith. She sat on the strip of rag carpeting that partially covered the rough floor, and drew on her stockings and her copper-

22

toed shoes. "Oh, sister, my fingers shake so I can't get the strings through the eyelets! Do you think Mr. Hoover might oversleep hisself? It can't help bein' nice—nicer'n I expect. Of course," she added, with a momentary regret, "I wish I had some other dress besides that buff calico, but I ain't, an' so—it's reel pretty, anyways, sister, ain't it?"

"Yes, Pet," said the girl gently. There was a bitter pity for the child in her heart.

"To think o' ridin' in the Libraty Car!" continued Esther, struggling with the shoe strings. "Course they'll let me. Paw knows the storekeeper, and Mr. Hoover kin tell 'em who I am. An' the horses, an' the ribbons, an' the music—an' all the little girls my age! Sister, it's awful never to have any little girls to play with! I guess maw don't know how I've wanted 'em, or she'd of took me to town sometimes. I ain't never been anywheres—except to Mis' Bunnels's fun'ral, when the minister prayed so long," she added, with a pious after-thought.

It was a happy child that was lifted to the back of the most trustworthy of the plow-horses to be escorted to the celebration by "Mr. Hoover," the hired man. The face under the cheap straw hat, with its wreath of pink and green artificial flowers, was almost pathetically radiant. To that poor little heart so hungry for pleasure, there could be no bliss so supreme as a ride in the village "Libraty Car"—to be one of the states, preferably "Oregon !" To hear the music and hold a flag, and sit close to little girls of her own age who would smile kindly at her and, perhaps, even ask her name shyly, and take her home with them to see their dolls.

"Oh," she cried, grasping the reins in her thin hands, "I'm all of a tremble ! Just like maw on wash days ! Only I ain't tired—I'm just glad."

There were shifting groups of children in front of the school house. Everything—even the white houses with their green blinds and neat dooryards—seemed strange and over-powering to Esther. The buoyancy with which she had surveyed the world from the back of a tall horse gave way to sudden timidity and self-consciousness.

Mr. Hoover put her down in the midst of the children. "There, now," he said cheerfully, "play around with the little girls like a nice body while I put up the horses."

A terrible loneliness came upon Esther as she watched him leading away the horses. All those merry children chattering and shouting, and not one speaking to her or taking the slightest notice of her. She realized with a suddenness that dazed her and blurred everything before her country eyes that she was very, very different from them—why, every one of the little girls was

24

dressed in pure, soft white, with a beautiful sash and bows; all wore pretty slippers. There was not one copper-toed shoe among them !

Her heart came up into her thin, little throat and beat and beat there. She wished that she might sit down and hide her shoes, but then the dress was just as bad. *That* couldn't be hidden. So she stood awkwardly in their midst, stiff and motionless, with a look in her eyes that ought to have touched somebody's heart.

Then the "Liberty Car" came, drawn by six noble white horses decorated with flags, ribbons and rosettes, and stepping out oh, so proudly in perfect time with the village band. Esther forgot her buff calico dress and her copper-toed shoes in the exquisite delight of that moment.

The little girls were placed in the car. Each carried a banner on which was painted the name of a state. What graceful, dancing little bodies they were, and how their feet twinkled and could not be quiet ! When "Oregon" went proudly by, Esther's heart sank. She wondered which state they would give to her.

The band stopped playing. All the girls were seated; somehow there seemed to be no place left for another. Esther went forward bravely and set one copper-toed shoe on the step of the car. The ladies in charge looked at her; then, at each other.

"Hello, Country!" cried a boy's shrill voice behind her suddenly. "My stars! She thinks she's goin' in the car. What a jay!"

Esther stood as if petrified with her foot still on the step. She felt that they were all looking at her. What terrible things human eyes can be! A kind of terror took hold of her. She trembled. There seemed to be a great stillness about her.

"Can't I go?" she said to one of the ladies. Her heart was beating so hard and so fast in her throat that her voice sounded far away to her. "My paw knows Mr. Mallory, the store-keeper. We live down by the river on the Nesley place. We're poor, but my paw alwus pays his debts. I come with Mr. Hoover; he's gone to put up the horses."

It was spoken—the poor little speech, at once passionate and despairing as any prayer to God. Then it was that Esther learned that there are silences which are harder to bear than the wildest tumult.

But presently one of the ladies said, very kindly—"Why, I am so sorry, little girl, but you see —er— all the little girls who ride in the car must —er—be dressed in white."

Esther removed her foot heavily from the step and stood back.

"Oh, look!" cried "Oregon", leaning from the

26

car. "She wanted to ride *in here* ! In a yellow calico dress and copper-toed shoes ! "

Then the band played, the horses pranced and tossed their heads, the flags and banners floated on the breeze, and the beautiful car moved away.

Esther stood looking after it until she heard Mr. Hoover's voice at her side. "W'y, what a funny little girl ! There the car's gone, an' she didn't go an' git in it, after all ! Did anybody ever see sech a funny little girl ? After gittin' up so airly, an' hurryin' everybody so for fear she'd be late, an' a-talkin' about ridin' in the Libraty Car for months—an' then to go an' not git in it after all ! "

Esther turned with a bursting heart. She threw herself passionately into his arms and hid her face on his breast.

"I want to go home," she sobbed. "Oh, I want to go home ! "

27

THE BLOW-OUT AT JENKINS'S GROCERY

THE BLOW-OUT AT JENKINS'S GROCERY

The hands of the big, round clock in Mr. Jenkins's grocery store pointed to eleven. Mr. Jenkins was tying a string around a paper bag containing a dollar's worth of sugar. He held one end of the string between his teeth. His three clerks were going around the store with little stiff prances of deference to the customers they were serving. It was the night before Christmas. They were all so worn out that their attempts at smiles were only painful contortions.

Mr. Jenkins looked at the clock. Then his eyes went in a hurried glance of pity to a woman sitting on a high stool close to the window. Her feet were drawn up on the top rung, and her thin shoulders stooped over her chest. She had sunken cheeks and hollow eyes; her cheek-bones stood out sharply.

For two hours she had sat there almost motionless. Three times she had lifted her head and fixed a strained gaze upon Mr. Jenkins and asked, "D'yuh want to shet up?" Each time, receiving an answer in the negative, she had sunk back into the same attitude of brute-like waiting.

It was a wild night. The rain drove its long,

slanting lances down the window-panes. The wind howled around corners, banged loose shutters, creaked swinging sign-boards to and fro, and vexed the telephone wires to shrill, continuous screaming. Fierce gusts swept in when the door was opened.

Christmas shoppers came and went. The woman saw nothing inside the store. Her eyes were set on the doors of a brightly lighted saloon across the street.

It was a small, new "boom" town on Puget Sound. There was a saloon on every corner, and a brass band in every saloon. The "establishment" opposite was having its "opening" that night. "At home" cards in square envelopes had been sent out to desirable patrons during the previous week. That day, during an hour's sunshine, a yellow chariot, drawn by six cream-colored horses with snow-white manes and tails, had gone slowly through the streets, bearing the members of the band clad in white and gold. It was followed by three open carriages, gay with the actresses who were to dance and sing that night on the stage in the rear of the saloon. All had yellow hair and were dressed in yellow with white silk sashes, and white ostrich plumes falling to their shoulders. It was a gorgeous procession, and it "drew."

The woman lived out in the Grand View addition. The addition consisted mainly of cabins built of "shakes" and charred stumps. The grand view was to come some ten or twenty years later on, when the forests surrounding the addition had taken their departure. It was a full mile from the store.

She had walked in with her husband through the rain and slush after putting six small children to bed. They were very poor. Her husband was shiftless. It was whispered of them by their neighbors that they couldn't get credit for "two bits" except at the saloons.

A relative had sent the woman ten dollars for a Christmas gift. She had gone wild with joy. Ten dollars! It was wealth. For once the children should have a real Christmas—a good dinner, toys, candy! Of all things, there should be a wax doll for the little girl who had cried for one every Christmas, and never even had one in her arms. Just for this one time they should be happy—like other children; and she should be happy in their happiness—like other mothers. What did it matter that she had only two calico dresses and one pair of shoes, half-soled at that, and capped across the toes?

Her husband had entered into her childish joy. He was kind and affectionate—when he was sober. That was why she had never had the heart to leave him. He was one of those men who are always needing, pleading for—and, alas! receiving—forgiveness; one of those men whom their women love passionately and cling to forever.

He promised her solemnly that he would not drink a drop that Christmas—so solemnly that she believed him. He had helped her to wash the dishes and put the children to bed. And he had kissed her.

Her face had been radiant when they came into Mr. Jenkins's store. That poor, gray face with its sunken cheeks and eyes! They bought a turkey—and with what anxious care she had selected it, testing its tenderness, balancing it on her bony hands, examining the scales with keen, narrowed eyes when it was weighed; and a quart of cranberries, a can of mince meat and a can of plum pudding, a head of celery, a pint of Olympia oysters, candy, nuts—and then the toys! She trembled with eagerness. Her husband stood watching her, smiling good-humoredly, his hands in his pockets. Mr. Jenkins indulged in some serious speculation as to where the money was coming from to pay for all this "blow-out". He set his lips together and resolved that the "blow-out" should not leave the store, under any amount of promises, until the cash paying for it was in his cash-drawer.

Suddenly the band began to play across the street. The man threw up his head like an old war-horse at the sound of a bugle note. A fire came into his eyes; into his face a flush of excitement. He walked down to the window and stood looking out, jingling some keys in his pocket. He breathed quickly.

After a few moments he went back to his wife. Mr. Jenkins had stepped away to speak to another customer.

"Say, Molly, old girl," he said affectionately, without looking at her, "yuh can spare me enough out o' that tenner to git a plug o' tobaccer for Christmas, can't yuh?"

"W'y—I guess so" said she slowly. The first cloud fell on her happy face.

"Well, jest let me have it, an' I'll run out an' be back before yuh're ready to pay for these here things. I'll only git two bits' worth."

She turned very pale.

"Can't yuh git it here, Mart?"

"No," he said in a whisper; "his'n ain't fit to chew. I'll be right back, Molly—honest."

She stood motionless, her eyes cast down, thinking. If she refused, he would be angry and remain away from home all the next day to pay her for the insult. If she gave it to him—well, she would have to take the chances. But oh, her hand shook as she drew the small gold piece from her shabby purse and reached it to him. His big, warm hand closed over it.

She looked up at him. Her eyes spoke the passionate prayer that her lips could not utter.

"Don't stay long, Mart," she whispered, not daring to say more.

"I won't, Molly," he whispered back. "I'll hurry up. Git anything yuh want."

She finished her poor shopping. Mr. Jenkins wrapped everything up neatly. Then he rubbed his hands together and looked at her, and said: "Well, there now, Mis' Dupen."

"I—jest lay 'em all together there on the counter," she said hesitatingly. "I'll have to wait till Mart comes back before I can pay yuh."

"I see him go into the s'loon over there," piped out the errand boy shrilly.

At the end of half an hour she climbed upon the high stool and fixed her eyes upon the saloon opposite and sat there.

She saw nothing but the glare of those windows and the light streaming out when the doors opened. She heard nothing but the torturing blare of the music. After awhile something commenced beating painfully in her throat and temples. Her limbs grew stiff—she was scarcely conscious that they ached. Once she shuddered strongly, as dogs do when they lie in the cold, waiting.

At twelve o'clock Mr. Jenkins touched her kindly on the arm. She looked up with a start.

36

Her face was gray and old; her eyes were almost wild in their strained despair.

"I guess I'll have to shet up now, Mis' Dupen," he said apologetically. "I'm sorry—"

She got down from the stool at once. "I can't take them things," she said, almost whispering. "I hate to of put yuh to all that trouble of doin' 'em up. I thought—but I can't take 'em. I hope yuh won't mind—very much." Her bony fingers twisted together under her thin shawl.

"Oh, that's all right," said Mr. Jenkins in an embarrassed way. She moved stiffly to the door. He put out the lights and followed her. He felt mean, somehow. For one second he hesitated, then he locked the door, and gave it a shake to make sure that it was all right.

"Well," he said, "good night. I wish you a mer—"

"Good night," said the woman. She was turning away when the doors of the saloon opened for two or three men to enter. The music, which had ceased for a few minutes, struck up another air—a familiar air.

She burst suddenly into wild and terrible laughter. "Oh, my Lord," she cried out, "they're a-playin' 'Home, Sweet Home!' *In there!* Oh, my Lord! *Wouldn't that kill yuh!*"

THE TAKIN' IN OF OLD MIS' LANE

THE TAKIN' IN OF OLD MIS' LANE

"Huhy! Huhy! Pleg take that muley cow! Huhy!"

"What she doin', maw?"

"Why, she's just a-holdin' her head over the bars, an' a-bawlin'! Tryin' to get into the little correll where her ca'f is! I wish paw 'd of done as I told him an' put her into the up meadow. If there's anything on earth I abominate it's to hear a cow bawl."

Mrs. Bridges gathered up several sticks of wood from the box in the corner by the stove, and going out into the yard, threw them with powerful movements of her bare arm in the direction of the bars. The cow lowered her hornless head and shook it defiantly at her, but held her ground. Isaphene stood in the open door, laughing. She was making a cake. She beat the mixture with a long-handled tin spoon while watching the fruitless attack. She had reddish brown hair that swept away from her brow and temples in waves so deep you could have lost your finger in any one of them; and good, honest gray eyes, and a mouth that was worth kissing. She wore a blue cotton gown that looked as if it had just left the ironing-table. Her sleeves were rolled to her elbows.

"It don't do any good, maw," she said, as her mother returned with a defeated air. "She just bawls an' shakes her head right in your face. Look at her!"

"Oh, I don't want to look at her. It seems to me your paw might of drove her to the up meadow, seein's he was goin' right up by there. It ain't like as if he'd of had to go out o' his way. It aggravates me offul."

She threw the last stick of wood into the box, and brushed the tiny splinters off her arm and sleeves.

"Well, I guess I might as well string them beans for dinner before I clean up."

She took a large milkpan, filled with beans, from the table and sat down near the window.

"Isaphene," she said, presently, "what do you say to an organ, an' a horse an' buggy? A horse with some style about him, that you could ride or drive, an' that 'u'd always be up when you wanted to go to town!"

"What do I say?" The girl turned and looked at her mother as if she feared one of them had lost her senses; then she returned to her cake-beating with an air of good-natured disdain.

"Oh, you can smile an' turn your head on one side, but you'll whistle another tune before long—

or I'll miss my guess. Isaphene, I've been savin' up chicken an' butter money ever since we come to Puget Sound ; then I've always got the money for the strawberry crop, an' for the geese an' turkeys, an' the calves, an' so on. Your paw's been real good about such things."

"I don't call it bein' good," said Isaphene. "Why shouldn't he let you have the money? You planted, an' weeded, an' picked the straw-berries ; an' you fed an' set the chickens, an' gethered the eggs ; an' you've had all the tendin' of the geese an' turkeys an' calves—to say nothin' of the cows bawlin' over the bars," she added, with a sly laugh. "I'd say you only had your rights when you get the money for such things."

"Oh, yes, that's fine talk." Mrs. Bridges nodded her head with an air of experience. "But it ain't all men-folks that gives you your rights ; so when one does, I say he deserves credit."

"Well, I wouldn't claim anybody 'd been good to me just because he give me what I'd worked for an' earned. Now, if he'd give you all the money from the potato patch every year, or the hay meadow, or anything he'd done all the work-in' with himself—I'd call that good in him. He never done anything like that, did he?"

"No, he never," replied Mrs. Bridges, testily. "An' what's more, he ain't likely to—nor any other man I know of! If you get a man that

43

gives you all you work for an' earn, you'll be lucky—with all your airs!''

"Well, I guess I'll manage to get my rights, somehow," said Isaphene, beginning to butter the cake-pan.

"Somebody's comin'!" exclaimed her mother, lowering her voice to a mysterious whisper.

"Who is it?" Isaphene stood up straight, with that little quick beating of mingled pleasure and dismay that the cry of company brings to country hearts.

"I can't see. I don't want to be caught peepin'. I can see it's a woman, though; she's just passin' the row of hollyhocks. Can't you stoop down an' peep? She won't see you 'way over there by the table."

Isaphene stooped and peered cautiously through the wild cucumber vines that rioted over the kitchen window.

"Oh, it's Mis' Hanna!"

"My goodness! An' the way this house looks! You'll have to bring her out here 'n the kitchen, too. I s'pose she's come to spend the day—she's got her bag with her, ain't she?"

"Yes. What'll we have for dinner? I ain't goin' to cut this cake for her. I want this for Sund'y."

"Why, we've got corn beef to boil, an' a head o' cabbage; an' these here beans; an', of course, potatoes; an' watermelon perserves. An' you can make a custard pie. I guess that's a good enough dinner for her. There! She's knockin'. Open the door, can't you? Well, if I ever! Look at that grease-spot on the floor!"

"Well, I didn't spill it."

"Who did, then, missy?"

"Well, *I* never."

Isaphene went to the front door, returning presently with a tall, thin lady.

"Here's Mis' Hanna, maw," she said, with the air of having made a pleasant discovery. Mrs. Bridges got up, greatly surprised, and shook hands with her visitor with exaggerated delight.

"Well, I'll declare! It's really you, is it? At last! Well, set right down an' take off your things. Isaphene, take Mis' Hanna's things. My! ain't it warm, walkin'?"

"It is so." The visitor gave her bonnet to Isaphene, dropping her black mitts into it after rolling them carefully together. "But it's always nice an' cool in your kitchen." Her eyes wandered about with a look of unabashed curiosity that took in everything. "I brought my crochet with me."

"I'm glad you did. You'll have to excuse the looks o' things. Any news?"

"None perticular." Mrs. Hanna began to crochet, holding the work close to her face. "Ain't it too bad about poor, old Mis' Lane?"

"What about her?" Mrs. Bridges snapped a bean-pod into three pieces, and looked at her visitor with a kind of pleased expectancy—as if almost any news, however dreadful, would be welcome as a relief to the monotony of existence. "Is she dead?"

"No, she ain't dead; but the poor, old creature 'd better be. She's got to go to the poor-farm, after all."

There was silence in the big kitchen, save for the rasp of the crochet needle through the wool and the snapping of the beans. A soft wind came in the window and drummed with the lightest of touches on Mrs. Bridges's temples. It brought all the sweets of the old-fashioned flower-garden with it—the mingled breaths of mignonette, stock, sweet lavender, sweet peas and clove pinks. The whole kitchen was filled with the fragrance. And what a big, cheerful kitchen it was! Mrs. Bridges contrasted it unconsciously with the poor-farm kitchen, and almost shivered, warm though the day was.

"What's her childern about?" she asked, sharply.

"Oh, her childern!" replied Mrs. Hanna, with a contemptuous air. "What does her childern amount to, I'd like to know."

46

"Her son 's got a good, comf'table house an' farm."

"Well, what if he has? He got it with his wife, didn't he? An' M'lissy won't let his poor, old mother set foot inside the house ! I don't say she is a pleasant body to have about—she's cross an' sick most all the time, an' childish. But that ain't sayin' her childern oughtn't to put up with her disagreeableness."

"She's got a married daughter, ain't she?"

"Yes, she's got a married daughter." Mrs. Hanna closed her lips tightly together and looked as if she might say something, if she chose, that would create a sensation.

"Well, ain't she got a good enough home to keep her mother in ?"

"Yes, she has. But she got *her* home along with her husband, an' he won't have the old soul any more 'n M'lissy would."

There was another silence. Isaphene had put the cake in the oven. She knelt on the floor and opened the door very softly now and then, to see that it was not browning too fast. The heat of the oven had crimsoned her face and arms.

"Guess you'd best put a piece o' paper on top o' that cake," said her mother. "It smells kind o' burny like."

"It's all right, maw."

Mrs. Bridges looked out the window.

Ain't my flowers doin' well, though, Mis' Hanna?"

"They are that. When I come up the walk I couldn't help thinkin' of poor, old Mis' Lane."

"What's that got to do with her?" Resentment bristled in Mrs. Bridges's tone and look.

Mrs. Hanna stopped crocheting, but held her hands stationary, almost level with her eyes, and looked over them in surprise at her questioner.

"Why, she ust to live here, you know."

"She did! In this house?"

"Why, yes. Didn't you know that? Oh, they ust to be right well off in her husband's time. I visited here consid'rable. My! the good things she always had to eat. I can taste 'em yet."

"Hunh! I'm sorry I can't give you as good as she did," said Mrs. Bridges, stiffly.

"Well, as if you didn't! You set a beautiful table, Mis' Bridges, an', what's more, that's your reputation all over. Everybody says that about you."

Mrs. Bridges smiled deprecatingly, with a slight blush of pleasure.

"They do, Mis' Bridges. I just told you about Mis' Lane because you'd never think it now of the poor, old creature. An' such flowers as she ust to have on both sides that walk! Lark-spurs, an' sweet-williams, an' bach'lor's-buttons, an' mournin'-widows, an' pumgranates, an' all kinds.

48

Guess you didn't know she set out that pink cab-
bage-rose at the north end o' the front porch, did
you ? An' that hop-vine that you've got trained
over your parlor window—set that out, too. An'
that row o' young alders between here an' the
barn—she set 'em all out with her own hands ; dug
the holes herself, an' all. It's funny she never
told you she lived here."

"Yes, it is," said Mrs. Bridges, slowly and
thoughtfully.

"It's a wonder to me she never broke down
an' cried when she was visitin' here. She can't
so much as mention the place without cryin'."

A dull red came into Mrs. Bridges's face.

"She never visited here."

"Never visited here !" Mrs. Hanna laid her
crochet and her hands in her lap, and stared.
"Why, she visited ev'rywhere. That's how she
managed to keep out o' the poor-house so long.
Ev'rybody was reel consid'rate about invitin' her.
But I expect she didn't like to come here because
she thought so much o' the place."

Isaphene looked over her shoulder at her
mother, but the look was not returned. The
beans were sputtering nervously into the pan.

"Ain't you got about enough, maw?" she
said. "That pan seems to be gettin' hefty."

"Yes, I guess." She got up, brushing the
strings off her apron, and set the pan on the

table. "I'll watch the cake now, Isaphene. You put the beans on in the pot to boil. Put a piece o' that salt pork in with 'em. Better get 'em on right away. It's pretty near eleven. Ain't this oven too hot with the door shet?"

Then the pleasant preparations for dinner went on. The beans soon commenced to boil, and an appetizing odor floated through the kitchen. The potatoes were pared—big, white fellows, smooth and long—with a sharp, thin knife, round and round and round, each without a break until the whole paring had curled itself about Isaphene's pretty arm almost to the elbow. The cabbage was chopped finely for the cold-slaw, and the vinegar and butter set on the stove in a saucepan to heat. Then Mrs. Bridges "set" the table, covering it first with a red cloth having a white border and fringe. In the middle of the table she placed an uncommonly large, six-bottled caster.

"I guess you'll excuse a red tablecloth, Mis' Hanna. The men-folks get their shirt-sleeves so dirty out in the fields that you can't keep a white one clean no time."

"I use red ones myself most of the time," replied Mrs. Hanna, crocheting industriously. "It saves washin'. I guess poor Mis' Lane 'll have to see the old place after all these years, whether she wants or not. They'll take her right past here to the poor-farm."

Mrs. Bridges set on the table a white plate holding a big square of yellow butter, and stood looking through the open door, down the path with its tall hollyhocks and scarlet poppies on both sides. Between the house and the barn some wild mustard had grown, thick and tall, and was now drifting, like a golden cloud, against the pale blue sky. Butterflies were throbbing through the air, and grasshoppers were crackling everywhere. It was all very pleasant and peaceful; while the comfortable house and barns, the wide fields stretching away to the forest, and the cattle feeding on the hillside added an appearance of prosperity. Mrs. Bridges wondered how she herself would feel—after having loved the place—riding by to the poor-farm. Then she pulled herself together and said, sharply:

"I'm afraid you feel a draught, Mis' Hanna, a-settin' so clost to the door."

"Oh, my, no; I like it. I like lots o' fresh air. Can't get it any too fresh for me. If I didn't have six childern an' my own mother to keep, I'd take her myself."

"Take who?" Mrs. Bridges's voice rasped as she asked the question. Isaphene paused on her way to the pantry, and looked at Mrs. Hanna with deeply thoughtful eyes.

"Why, Mis' Lane—who else?—before I'd let her go to the poor-farm."

" Well, I think her childern ought to be *made* to take care of her!" Mrs. Bridges went on setting the table with brisk, angry movements. "That's what I think about it. The law ought to take holt of it."

"Well, you see the law *has* took holt of it," said Mrs. Hanna, with a grim smile. "It seems a shame that there ain't somebody in the neighborhood that 'u'd take her in. She ain't much expense, but a good deal o' trouble. She's sick, in an' out o' bed, nigh onto all the time. My opinion is she's been soured by all her troubles; an' that if somebody 'u'd only take her in an' be kind to her, her temper'ment 'u'd emprove up wonderful. She's always mighty grateful for ev'ry little chore you do her. It just makes my heart ache to think o' her a-havin' to go to the poor-house!"

Mrs. Bridges lifted her head; all the softness and irresolution went out of her face.

"Well, I'm sorry for her," she said, with an air of dismissing a disagreeable subject; "but the world's full o' troubles, an' if you cried over all o' them you'd be a-cryin' all the time. Isaphene, you go out an' blow that dinner-horn. I see the men-folks 'av' got the horses about foddered. What did you do?" she cried out, sharply. "Drop a smoothin'-iron on your hand? Well,

5?

my goodness! Why don't you keep your eyes about you? You'll go an' get a cancer yet!"

"I'm thinkin' about buyin' a horse an' buggy," she announced, with stern triumph, when the girl had gone out. "An' an organ. Isaphene's been wantin' one most offul. I've give up her paw's ever gettin' her one. First a new harrow, an' then a paten' rake, an' then a seed-drill—an' then my mercy"—imitating a musculine voice—"he ain't got any money left for silliness! But I've got some laid by. I'd like to see his eyes when he comes home an' finds a bran new buggy with a top an' all, an' a horse that he can't hetch to a plow, no matter how bad he wants to! I ain't sure but I'll get a phaeton."

"They ain't so strong, but they're handy to get in an' out of—'specially for old, trembly knees."

"I ain't so old that I'm trembly!"

"Oh, my—no," said Mrs. Hanna, with a little start. "I was just thinkin' mebbe sometimes you'd go out to the poor-farm an' take poor, old Mis' Lane for a little ride. It ain't more'n five miles from here, is it? She ust to have a horse an' buggy o' her own. Somehow, I can't get her off o' my mind at all to-day. I just heard about her as I was a-startin' for your house."

The men came to the house. They paused on the back porch to clean their boots on the scraper

53

and wash their hands and faces with water dipped
from the rain-barrel. Their faces shone like
brown marble when they came in.

It was five o'clock when Mrs. Hanna, with a
sigh, began rolling the lace she had crocheted
around the spool, preparatory to taking her departure.

"Well," she said, "I must go. I had no idy
it was so late. How the time does go, a-talkin'.
I've had a right nice time. Just see how well
I've done—crocheted full a yard since dinner-
time ! My ! how pretty that hop-vine looks. It
makes awful nice shade, too. I guess when Mis'
Lane planted it she thought she'd be settin' under
it herself to-day—she took such pleasure in it."

The ladies were sitting on the front porch. It
was cool and fragrant out there. The shadow of
the house reached almost to the gate now. The
bees had been drinking too many sweets—greedy
fellows !—and were lying in the red poppies, dron-
ing stupidly. A soft wind was blowing from Puget Sound and turning over the clover leaves,
making here a billow of dark green and there one
of light green ; it was setting loose the perfume
of the blossoms, too, and sifting silken thistle-
needles through the air. Along the fence was a

hedge, eight feet high, of the beautiful ferns that grow luxuriantly in western Washington. The pasture across the lane was a tangle of royal color, being massed in with golden-rod, fire-weed, steeple-bush, yarrow, and large field-daisies; the cotton-woods that lined the creek at the side of the house were snowing. Here and there the sweet twin-sister of the steeple-bush lifted her pale and fluffy plumes; and there was one lovely, lavender company of wild asters.

Mrs. Bridges arose and followed her guest into the spare bedroom.

"When they goin' to take her to the poor-farm?" she asked, abruptly.

"Day after to-morrow. Ain't it awful? It just makes me sick. I couldn't of eat a bite o' dinner if I'd stayed at home, just for thinkin' about it. They say the poor, old creature ain't done nothin' but cry an' moan ever since she knowed she'd got to go."

"Here's your bag," said Mrs. Bridges. "Do you want I should tie your veil?"

"No, thanks; I guess I won't put it on. If I didn't have such a big fam'ly an' my own mother to keep, I'd take her in myself before I'd see her go to the poor-house. If I had a small fam'ly an' plenty o' room, I declare my conscience wouldn't let me sleep nights."

A deep red glow spread over Mrs. Bridges's face.

"Well, I guess you needn't to keep a-hintin' for me to take her," she said, sharply.

"*You!*" Mrs. Hanna uttered the word in a tone that was an unintentional insult; in fact, Mrs. Bridges affirmed afterward that her look of astonishment, and, for that matter, her whole air of dazed incredulity were insulting. "I never once thought o' *you*," she said, with an earnestness that could not be doubted.

"Why not o' me?" demanded Mrs. Bridges, showing something of her resentment. "What you been talkin' an' harpin' about her all day for, if you wasn't hintin' for me to take her in?"

"I never thought o' such a thing," repeated her visitor, still looking rather helplessly dazed. "I talked about it because it was on my mind, heavy, too; an', I guess, because I wanted to talk my conscience down."

Mrs. Bridges cooled off a little and folded her hands over the bedpost.

"Well, if you wasn't hintin'," she said, in a conciliatory tone, "it's all right. You kep' harpin' on the same string till I thought you was; an' it riles me offul to be hinted at. I'll take anything right out to my face, so's I can answer it, but I won't be hinted at. "But why"—having rid herself of the grievance she at once swung

56

around to the insult—"why *didn't* you think o'
me?"

Mrs. Hanna cleared her throat and began to
unroll her mitts.

"Well, I don't know just why," she replied,
helplessly. She drew the mitts on, smoothing
them well up over her thin wrists. "I don't know
why, I'm sure. I'd thought o' most ev'rybody
in the neighborhood—but you never come into
my head *onct*. I was as innocent o' hintin' as a
babe unborn."

Mrs. Bridges drew a long breath noiselessly.

"Well," she said, absent-mindedly, "come
again, Mis' Hanna. An' be sure you always
fetch your work an' stay the afternoon."

"Well, I will. But it's your turn to come
now. Where's Isaphene?"

"I guess she's makin' a fire 'n the cook-stove
to get supper by."

"Well, tell her to come over an' stay all night
with Julia some night."

"Well—I will."

Mrs. Bridges went into the kitchen and sat
down, rather heavily, in a chair. Her face wore
a puzzled expression.

"Isaphene, did you hear what we was a-sayin'
in the bedroom?"

"Yes, most of it, I guess."

"Well, what do you s'pose was the reason she

57

never thought o' me a-takin' Mis' Lane in? Says she'd thought o' ev'rybody else."

"Why, you never thought o' takin' her in yourself, did you?" said Isaphene, turning down the damper of the stove with a clatter. "I don't see how anybody else 'u'd think of it when you didn't yourself."

"Well, don't you think it was offul impadent in her to say that, anyhow?"

"No, I don't. She told the truth."

"Why ought they to think o' ev'rybody takin' her exceptin' me, I'd like to know."

"Because ev'rybody else, I s'pose, has thought of it theirselves. The neighbors have all been chippin' in to help her for years. You never done nothin' for her, did you? You never invited her to visit here, did you?"

"No, I never. But that ain't no sayin' I wouldn't take her as quick 's the rest of 'em. They ain't none of 'em takin' her in very fast, be they?"

"No, they ain't," said Isaphene, facing her mother with a steady look. "They ain't a one of 'em but 's got their hands full—no spare room, an' lots o' childern or their folks to take care of."

"Hunh!" said Mrs. Bridges. She began chopping cold boiled beef for hash.

"I don't believe I'll sleep to-night for thinkin' about it," she said, after a while.

"I won't neither, maw. I wish she wasn't goin' right by here."

"So do I."

After a long silence Mrs. Bridges said—"I don't suppose your paw'd hear to us a-takin' her in."

"I guess he'd hear to 't if we would," said Isaphene, dryly.

"Well, we can't do't; that's all there is about it," announced Mrs. Bridges, with a great air of having made up her mind. Isaphene did not reply. She was slicing potatoes to fry, and she seemed to agree silently with her mother's decision. Presently, however, Mrs. Bridges said, in a less determined tone—"There's no place to put her in, exceptin' the spare room—an' we can't get along without that, noways."

"No," said Isaphene, in a non-committal tone.

Mrs. Bridges stopped chopping and looked thoughtfully out of the door.

"There's this room openin' out o' the kitchen," she said, slowly. "It's nice an' big an' sunny. It 'u'd be handy 'n winter, bein' right off o' the kitchen. But it ain't furnished up."

"No," said Isaphene, "it ain't."

"An' I know your paw'd never furnish it."

Isaphene laughed. "No, I guess not," she said.

"Well, there's no use a-thinkin' about it, Isaphene; we just can't take her. Better get them potatoes on; I see the men-folks comin' up to the barn."

The next morning after breakfast Isaphene said suddenly, as she stood washing dishes— "Maw, I guess you'd better take the organ money an' furnish up that room."

Mrs. Bridges turned so sharply she dropped the turkey-wing with which she was polishing the stove.

"You don't never mean it," she gasped.

"Yes, I do. I know we'd both feel better to take her in than to take in an organ"—they both laughed rather foolishly at the poor joke. "You can furnish the room real comf'table with what it 'u'd take to buy an organ; an' we can get the horse an' buggy, too."

"Oh, Isaphene, I've never meant but what you should have an organ. I know you'd learn fast. You'd soon get so's you could play 'Lilly Dale' an' 'Hazel Dell;' an' you might get so's you could play 'General Persifer F. Smith's Grand March.' No, I won't never spend that money for nothin' but an organ — so you can just shet up about it."

"I want a horse an' buggy worse, maw," said Isaphene, after a brief but fierce struggle with the dearest desire of her heart. "We can get a horse that I can ride, too. An' we'll get a

60

phaeton, so's we can take Mis' Lane to church an' around." Then she added, with a regular masterpiece of diplomacy—"We'll show the neighbors that when we do take people in, we take 'em in all over!"

"Oh, Isaphene," said her mother, weakly, "wouldn't it just astonish 'em!"

It was ten o'clock of the following morning when Isaphene ran in and announced that she heard wheels coming up the lane. Mrs. Bridges paled a little and breathed quickly as she put on her bonnet and went out to the gate.

A red spring-wagon was coming slowly toward her, drawn by a single, bony horse. The driver was half asleep on the front seat. Behind, in a low chair, sat old Mrs. Lane; she was stooping over, her elbows on her knees, her gray head bowed.

Mrs. Bridges held up her hand, and the driver pulled in the unreluctant horse.

"How d'you do, Mis' Lane? I want that you should come in an' visit me a while."

The old creature lifted her trembling head and looked at Mrs. Bridges; then she saw the old house, half hidden by vines and flowers, and her dim eyes filled with bitter tears.

"We ain't got time to stop, ma'am," said the driver, politely. "I'm a takin' her to the county," he added, in a lower tone, but not so low that the old woman did not hear.

"You'll have to make time," said Mrs. Bridges, bluntly. "You get down an' help her out. You don't have to wait. When I'm ready for her to go to the county, I'll take her myself."

Not understanding in the least, but realizing, as he said afterwards, that she "meant business" and wasn't the kind to be fooled with, the man obeyed with alacrity.

"Now, you lean all your heft on me," said Mrs. Bridges, kindly. She put her arm around the old woman and led her up the hollyhock path, and through the house into the pleasant kitchen.

"Isaphene, you pull that big chair over here where it's cool. Now, Mis' Lane, you set right down an' rest."

Mrs. Lane wiped the tears from her face with an old cotton handkerchief. She tried to speak, but the sobs had to be swallowed down too fast. At last she said, in a choked voice —"It's awful good in you — to let me see the old place — once more. The Lord bless you — for it. But I'm most sorry I stopped — seems now as if I — just *couldn't* go on."

"Well, you ain't goin' on," said Mrs. Bridges, while Isaphene went to the door and stood looking toward the hill with drowned eyes. "This is our little joke — Isaphene's an' mine. This'll be your home as long as it's our'n. An' you're goin' to have this nice big room right off o' the kitchen, as soon 's we can furnish it up. An' we're goin' to get a horse an' buggy — a *low* buggy, so's you can get in an' out easy like — an' take you to church an' all around."

That night, after Mrs. Bridges had put Mrs. Lane to bed and said good-night to her, she went out on the front porch and sat down; but presently, remembering that she had not put a candle in the room, she went back, opening the door noiselessly, not to disturb her. Then she stood perfectly still. The old creature had got out of bed and was kneeling beside it, her face buried in her hands.

"Oh, Lord God," she was saying aloud, "bless these kind people — bless 'em, oh, Lord God! Hear a poor, old mis'rable soul's prayer, an' bless 'em! An' if they've ever done a sinful thing, oh, Lord God, forgive 'em for it, because they've kep' me out o' the poor-house —"

Mrs. Bridges closed the door, and stood sobbing as if her heart must break.

"What's the matter, maw?" said Isaphene, coming up suddenly.

"Never you mind what's the matter," said her mother, sharply, to conceal her emotion. "You get to bed, an' don't bother your head about what's the matter of me."

Then she went down the hall and entered her own room; and Isaphene heard the key turned in the lock.

THE MANEUVERING OF MRS. SYBERT

THE MANEUVERING OF MRS. SYBERT

"Why, mother, where are you a-goin', all dressed up so?"

Mr. Sybert stood in the bedroom door and stared at his wife's ample back. There was a look of surprise in his blue eyes. Mrs. Sybert stooped before the bureau, and opened the middle drawer, taking hold of both handles and watching it carefully as she drew it toward her. Sometimes it came out crookedly; and every one knows that a drawer that opens crookedly, will, in time, strain and rub the best bureau ever made. From a red pasteboard box that had the picture of a pretty actress on the cover, Mrs. Sybert took a linen handkerchief that had been ironed until it shone like satin. After smoothing an imaginary wrinkle out of it, she put it into her pocket, set her bonnet a little further over her forehead, pushing a stray lock sternly where it belonged, adjusted her bonnet-strings, which were so wide and so stiff that they pressed her ears away from her head, giving her a bristling appearance, and buttoned her gloves with a hair-pin; then, having gained time and decided upon a reply, she said, cheerfully, "What's that, father?"

"Well, it took you a right smart spell to answer, didn't it? I say, where are you a-goin', all dressed up so?"

Mrs. Sybert took her black silk bag with round spots brocaded upon it, and put its ribbons leisurely over her arm. "I'm a-goin' to see Mis' Nesley," she said.

Her husband's face reddened. "What's that you say, mother? You're a-goin' to do *what?* I reckon I'm a-goin' a little deef."

"I'm a-goin' to see Mis' Nesley." Mrs. Sybert spoke calmly. No one would have suspected that she was reproaching herself for not getting out of the house ten minutes sooner. "He never'd 'a' heard a thing about it," she was thinking ; but she looked straight into his eyes. Her eyelids did not quiver.

The red in Mr. Sybert's face deepened. He stood in the door, so she could not pass. Indeed, she did not try. Mrs. Sybert had not studied signs for nothing during the thirty years she had been a wife. "I reckon you're a-foolin', mother," he said. "Just up to some o' your devilment !"

"No, I ain't up to no devilment, father," she said, still calmly. "You'd best let me by, now, so's I can go ; it's half after two."

"D' you mean to say that you're a-ne'rnest? A-talkin' about goin' to see that *hussy* of a Mis' Nesley?"

68

"Yes, I'm a-ne'rnest," said Mrs. Sybert, firmly. "She ain't a hussy, as I know of. What you got agin 'er, I'd like to know?"

"*I* ain't got anything agin 'er. Now, what's the sense o' you're a-pretendin' you don't know the talk about 'er, mother?" Mr. Sybert's tone had changed slightly. He did not like the poise of his wife's body; it bespoke determination — a fight to the finish if necessary. "You know she's be'n the town talk fer five years. Your own tawngue hez run on about 'er like's if 't was split in the middle an' loose at both en's. There wa'n't a woman in town that spoke to 'er"——

"There was men, though, that did," said Mrs. Sybert, calmly. "I rec'lect bein' in at Mis' Carney's one day, an' seein' you meet 'er opposite an' take off your hat to 'er — bowin' an' scrapin' right scrumptious like."

Mr. Sybert changed his position uneasily, and cleared his throat. "Well, that's diff'rent," he said. "I ust to know 'er before 'er husband died"——

"Well, I ust to know 'er, then, too," said Mrs. Sybert, quietly.

"Well, you hed to stop speakin' to 'er after she got to actin' up so, but it wa'n't so easy fer me to stop biddin' 'er the time o' day."

"Why not?" said Mrs. Sybert, stolidly.

"Why not!" repeated her husband, loudly; he

69

was losing his temper. "What's the sense o' your actin' the fool so, mother? Why, if I'd 'a' set myself up as bein' too virtjus to speak to 'er ev'ry man in town 'u'd 'a' be'n blagg'ardin' me about bein' so mighty good!"

"Why *sh'u'dn't* you be so mighty good, father? You expect me to be, I notice."

Mr. Sybert choked two or three times. His face was growing purplish.

"Oh, *damn!*" he burst out. Then he looked frightened. "Now, see here, mother! You're aggravatin' me awful. You know as well as me that men ain't expected to be as good all their lives as women"——

"Why ain't they expected to?" Mrs. Sybert's tone and look were stern.

"I don't know why they ain't, mother, but I know they *ain't* expected to — an' I know they ain't as *good*, 'ither." This last was a fine bit of diplomacy. But it was wasted.

"They ain't as good, aigh? Well, the reason they ain't as good is just because they ain't expected to be! That's just the reason. You can't get around that, can you, father?"

Evidently he could not.

"An' now," continued Mrs. Sybert, "that she's up an' married Mr. Nesley an' wants to live a right life, I'm a-goin' to see her."

"How d'you know she wants to live a right life?"

70

"I don't know it, father. I just *reckon* she does. When you wanted I sh'u'd marry you, my father shook his head, an' says—'Lucindy, I do' know what to say. John's be'n a mighty fast young fello' to give a good girl to fer the askin',' but I says—'Well, father, I reckon he wants to start in an' live a right life now.' An' so I reckon that about Mis' Nesley."

"God A'mighty, mother!" exclaimed Mr. Sybert, violently. "That's diff'rent. Them things ain't counted the same in men. Most all men nowadays sow their wild oats an' then settle down, an' ain't none the worse for it. It just helps 'em to appreciate good women, an' to make good husbands."

"Well, I reckon Mis' Nesley knows how to appreciate a good man by this time," said Mrs. Sybert, with unintentional irony. "I reckon she's got all her wild oats sowed, an' is ready to settle down an' make a good wife. So I'm goin' to see 'er. Let me by, father. I've fooled a ha'f an hour away now, when I'd ort to 'a' be'n on the road there."

"Now, see here, mother. You ain't goin' a step. The whole town 's excited over a nice man like Mr. Nesley a-throwin' hisself away on a no-account woman like her, an' you sha'n't be seen a-goin' there an' upholdin' her."

Mrs. Sybert looked long and steadily into her

husband's eyes. It was her policy to fight until she began to lose ground, and then to quietly turn her forces to maneuvering. "I reckon," she was now reflecting; "it's about time to begin maneuv'rin'."

"Well, father," she said, mildly; "I've made up my mind to go an' see Mis' Nesley an' encourage her same's I w'u'd any man that wanted to live better. An' I'm a-goin'."

"You *ain't* a-goin'!" thundered Mr. Sybert. "I forbid you to budge a step! You sha'n't disgrace yourself, Mrs. Sybert, if you do want to, while you're my wife!"

Mrs. Sybert untied her bonnet strings, and laid her bag on the foot of the bed. "All right, father," she said, "I won't go till you tell me I can. I always hev tried to do just as you wanted I sh'u'd."

She went into another room to take off her best dress. Mr. Sybert stood staring after her, speechless. He had the dazed look of a cat that falls from a great height and alights, uninjured, upon its feet. The maneuvering had commenced.

Mr. Sybert spent the afternoon at the postoffice grocery store. It was a pleasant place to sit. There was always a cheerful fire in the rusty box-stove in the back room, and there were barrels and odds and ends of chairs scattered around, whereon men who had an hour to squander might sit and talk over the latest scandal. Men, as it is well known, are above the petty gossip as to servants and best gowns which women enjoy ; but, without scruple or conscience, they will talk away a woman's character, even when they see her struggling to live down a misfortune or sin and begin a new life. There are many characters talked away in the back rooms of grocery stores.

It was six o'clock when he went home. As he went along the narrow plank walk, he thought of the good supper that would be awaiting him, and his heart softened to "mother."

"I reckon I was too set," he reflected. "There ain't many women as good an' faithful as mother. I don't see what got it into her head to go to see that Mis' Nesley—an' to talk up so to me. She never done that afore."

The door was locked. In surprise he fumbled about in the dark for the seventh flower-pot in the third row, where mother always hid the key. Yes, it was there. But his knees shook a little as he entered the house. He could not remember that he had ever found her absent at supper time since the children were married. Some of the neighbors must be sick. In that case she would have left a note ; and he lighted the kitchen candle, and searched for it. It was pinned to a cushion on the bureau in the bedroom. The house was cold, but he did not wait to kindle a fire.

He sat down by the bureau, and with fingers somewhat clumsier than usual, adjusted his spectacles over his high, thin nose. Then, leaning close to the candle, he read the letter, the composition of which must have given "mother" some anxious hours. It was written with painful precision.

"DEAR FATHER: You will find the coald meat in the safe out on the back porch in the stun crock covered up with a pie pan. The apple butter is in the big peory jar down in the seller with a plate and napkeen tied over it. Put them back on when you get some out so the ants wont get into. There's a punkin pie on the bottom shelf of the pantree to the right side of the door as you go in, and some coffy in the mill all ground. I'm offul sorry I hadent time to fix supper. I hev gone to Johns and Marias to stay tell you come after me and I don't want that you shud come tell you change your mind bout Mis Nesley, if it takes till dumesday to change it. I aint never gone against you in anythin before, but I haf to this time. Im goin to stay at Johns and Marias tell you come of yourself and get me. You dont haf to say nothin before John and Maria except just well mother Ive come after you. Then I'll know you meen I can go and see Mis Nesley.

Well father I reckon youll be surprised but Ive been thinkin bout that poor woman and us not givin her a chanse after what Christ said bout castin the first stun. He didnt make no difrence between mens and womens sins and I dont perpose to. There aint a woman alive thats worse than haff the men are when they conclud to settle down and live right and if you give men a chanse youve got to give women a chanse too. They both got

74

soles an I reckon thats what Gods thinkin bout. I married you and give you a chanse and I reckon youd best do as much fer Mis Nesley.

If you dont come fer me Ill live at Johns and Marias and I want that you shud keep all the things but the hit and miss rag carpet. I dont think I cud get along without that. Marias are all wove in stripes and look so comon. And my cloze and one fether bed and pillow. Well thats all.   MOTHER."

"I laid out your clean undercloze on the foot of the bed and your sox with them."

One fine afternoon the following week Mrs. Sybert, looking through the geraniums in Maria's kitchen window, saw her husband drive up to the gate. She did not look surprised.

"Here's father come to get me, Maria," she said, lifting her voice.

Maria came out of the pantry with flour on her hands and arms and stood waiting. Mr. Sybert came in, stamping, and holding his head high and stiffly. He had a lofty and condescending air.

"Well, mother," he said, "I've come after you."

"Well," said Mrs. Sybert, "set down till I get on my things. I've had a right nice vis't, but I'm glad to get home. Did you find the apple butter?"

On the road home Mrs. Sybert talked cheerfully about John and Maria and their domestic affairs. Mr. Sybert listened silently. He held his body

75

erect, looking neither to the right nor to the left. He did not speak until they approached Mr. Nesley's gate. Then he said, with firmness and dignity :

"Mother, I've b'en thinkin' that you'd best go an' see Mis' Nesley, after all. I changed my mind down at the postoffice groc'ry store that same afternoon an' went home, meanin' to tell you I wanted you sh'u'd go an' see 'er—but you was gone to John's an' Maria's. I reckon you'd best stop right now an' have it over."

"Well," said Mrs. Sybert.

She descended meekly over the front wheel. There was not the slightest air of triumph about her until she got inside the gate. Then a smile went slowly across her face. But her husband did not see it. He was looking out of the corners of his eyes at the house across the road. Mrs. Deacon, the druggist's wife, and all her children had their faces flattened against the window.

Mr. Sybert's determination kept his head high, but not his spirit.

"God A'mighty!" he groaned. "The whole town 'll know it to-morrow. I'd rather die than face that groc'ry store—after the way I've went on about people upholdin' of her !"

A POINT OF KNUCKLING-DOWN

A POINT OF KNUCKLING-DOWN

IN THREE PARTS

PART I

Emarine went along the narrow hall and passed through the open door. There was something in her carriage that suggested stubbornness. Her small body had a natural backward sway, and the decision with which she set her heels upon the floor had long ago caused the readers of character in the village to aver that "Emarine Endey was contrairier than any mule."

She wore a brown dress, a gray shawl folded primly around her shoulders, and a hat that tried in vain to make her small face plain. There was a frill of white, cheap lace at her slender throat, fastened in front with a cherry ribbon. Heavy gold earrings with long, shining pendants reached almost to her shoulders. They quivered and glittered with every movement.

Emarine was pretty, in spite of many freckles and the tightness with which she brushed her hair from her face and coiled it in a sleek knot at the back of her head. " Now, be sure you get it just so slick, Emarine," her mother would say, watching her steadily while she combed and brushed and twisted her long tresses.

As Emarine reached the door her mother followed her down the hall from the kitchen. The house was old, and two or three loose pieces in the flooring creaked as she stepped heavily upon them.

"Oh, say, Emarine!"

"Well?"

"You get an' bring home a dollar's worth o' granylated sugar, will you?"

"Well."

"An' a box o' ball bluin'. Mercy, child! Your dress-skirt sags awful in the back. Why don't you run a tuck in it?"

Emarine turned her head over her shoulder with a birdlike movement, and bent backward, trying to see the offensive sag.

"Can't you pin it up, maw?"

"Yes, I guess. Have you got a pin? Why, Emarine Endey! If ever I see in all my born days! What are you a-doin' with a red ribbon on you — an' your Uncle Herndon not cold in his grave yet! A fine spectickle you'd make o' yourself, a-goin' the length an' the breadth o' the town with that thing a-flarin' on you. You'll disgrace this whole fambly yet! I have to keep watch o' you like a two-year-old baby. Now, you get an' take it right off o' you; an' don't

you let me ketch you a-puttin' it on again till a
respectful time after he's be'n dead. I never
hear tell o' such a thing."

"I don't see what a red ribbon's got to do
with Uncle Herndon's bein' dead," said Emarine.

"Oh, you don't, aigh? Well, *I* see. You
act as if you didn't have no feelin'."

"Well, goin' without a red ribbon won't make
me feel any worse, will it, maw?"

"No, it won't. Emarine, what does get into
you to act so tantalizin'? I guess it 'll look a
little better. I guess the neighbors won't talk
quite so much. You can see fer yourself how
they talk about Mis' Henspeter because she wore
a rose to church before her husband had be'n
dead a year. All she had to say fer herself was
that she liked flowers, an' didn't sense it 'u'd be
any disrespect to her husband to wear it—seein's
he'd always liked 'em, too. They all showed
her 'n a hurry what they thought about it. She's
got narrow borders on all her han'kachers, too,
a'ready."

"Why don't you stay away from such people?"
said Emarine. "Old gossips! You know I
don't care what the neighbors say—or think,
either."

"Well, *I* do. The land knows they talk a
plenty even without givin' 'em anything to talk
about. You get an' take that red ribbon off o'
you."

"Oh, I'll take it off if you want I sh'u'd."
She unfastened it deliberately and laid it on a
little table. She had an exasperating air of being unconvinced and of complying merely for the
sake of peace.

She gathered her shawl about her shoulders
and crossed the porch.

"Emarine!"

"Well?"

"Who's that a-comin' over the hill path? I
can't make out the dress. It looks some like
Mis' Grandy, don't it?"

Emarine turned her head. Her eyelids quivered closer together in an effort to concentrate
her vision on the approaching guest.

"Well, I never!" exclaimed her mother, in
a subdued but irascible tone. "There you go—
a-lookin' right square at her, when I didn't want
that she sh'u'd know we saw her! It does seem
to me sometimes, Emarine, that you ain't got
good sense."

"I'd just as soon she knew we saw her," said
Emarine, unmoved. "It's Miss Presly, maw."

"Oh, land o' goodness! That old sticktight?
She'll stay all day if she stays a minute. Set
an' set! An' there I've just got the washin' all
out on the line, an' she'll tell the whole town we
wear underclo's made out o' unbleached muslin!"

82

Are you sure it's her? It don't look overly like her shawl."

"Yes, it's her."

"Well, go on an' stop an' talk to her, so 's to give me a chance to red up some. Don't ferget the ball bluin', Emarine."

Emarine went down the path and met the visitor just between the two tall lilac trees, whose buds were beginning to swell.

"Good mornin', Miss Presly."

"Why, good mornin', Emarine. Z' your maw to home?"

"Yes 'm."

"I thought I'd run down an' set a spell with her, an' pass the news."

Emarine smiled faintly and was silent.

"Ain't you goin' up town pretty early fer wash-day?"

"Yes 'm."

"I see you hed a beau home from church las' night."

Emarine's face flushed; even her ears grew rosy.

"Well, I guess he's a reel nice young man, anyways, Emarine. You needn't to blush so. Mis' Grandy was a-sayin' she thought you'd done offul well to git him. He owns the house an' lot they live in, an' he's got five hunderd dollars in the bank. I reckon he'll have to live with the

83

ol' lady, though, when he gits married. They do say she's turrable hard to suit."

Emarine lifted her chin. The gold pendants glittered like diamonds.

"It don't make any difference to me whuther she's hard to suit or easy," she said. "I'll have to be goin' on now. Just knock at the front door, Miss Presly."

"Oh, I can go right around to the back, just as well, an' save your maw the trouble o' comin' to the door. If she's got her washin' out, I can stoop right under the clo's line."

"Well, we like to have our comp'ny come to the front door," said Emarine, dryly.

It was a beautiful morning in early spring. The alders and the maples along the hill were wrapped in reddish mist. The saps were mounting through delicate veins. Presently the mist would quicken to a pale green as the young leaves unfolded, but as yet everything seemed to be waiting. The brown earth had a fresh, woody smell that caused the heart to thrill with a vague sense of ecstasy — of some delight deep hidden and inexplicable. Pale lavender "spring beauties" stood shyly in groups or alone, in sheltered places along the path. There was even, here and there, a trillium—or white lily, as the children called it—shivering on its slender stem. There were old stumps, too, hollowed out by long-spent

84

flames into rustic urns, now heaped to their ragged rims with velvet moss. On a fence near a meadow-lark was pouring out its few, but full and beautiful, notes of passion and desire. Emarine paused to listen. Her heart vibrated with exquisite pain to the ravishment of regret in those liquid tones.

"Sounds as if he was sayin'—'*Sweet—oh—Sweet—my heart is breaking!*'" she said; and then with a kind of shame of the sentiment in such a fancy, she went on briskly over the hill. Her heels clicked sharply on the hard road.

Before she reached the long wooden stairs which led from the high plateau down to the one street of Oregon City, Emarine passed through a beautiful grove of firs and cedars. Already the firs were taking on their little plushy tufts of pale green, and exuding a spicy fragrance. Occasionally a last year's cone drew itself loose and sunk noiselessly into a bed of its own brown needles. A little way from the path a woodpecker clung to a tree, hammering into the tough bark with its long beak. As Emarine approached, it flew heavily away, the undersides of its wings flashing a scarlet streak along the air.

As her eyes ceased following its flight, she became aware that some one was standing in the path, waiting. A deep, self-conscious blush swept over her face and throat. "Emarine never does anything up by halves," her mother was wont to declare. "When she blushes, she *blushes!*"

She stepped slowly toward him with a sudden stiff awkwardness.

"Oh—you, is it, Mr. Parmer?" she said, with an admirable attempt—but an attempt only—at indifference.

"Yes, it's me," said the young fellow, with an embarrassed laugh. With a clumsy shuffle he took step with her. Both faces were flaming. Emarine could not lift her eyes from their contemplation of the dead leaves in her path—yet she passed a whole company of "spring beauties" playing hide-and-seek around a stump, without seeing them. Her pulses seemed full of little hammers, beating away mercilessly. Her fingers fumbled nervously with the fringes on her shawl.

"Don't choo want I sh'u'd pack your umberell fer yuh?" asked the young man, solemnly.

"Why—yes, if you want."

It was a faded thing she held toward him, done up rather baggily, too ; but he received it as reverently as if it had been a twenty-dollar silk one with a gold handle.

"Does your mother know I kep' yuh comp'ny home from church last night?"

"Unh-hunh."

"What 'id she say?"

"She didn't say much."

86

"Well, what?"

"Oh, not much." Emarine was rapidly recovering her self-possession. "I went right in an' up an' told her."

· "Well, why can't choo tell me what she said? Emarine, yuh can be the contrairiest girl when yuh want."

"Can I?" She flashed a coquettish glance at him. She was quite at her ease by this time, although the color was still burning deep in her cheeks. "I sh'u'dn't think you'd waste so much time on contrary people, Mr. Parmer."

"Oh, Emarine, go on an' tell me!"

"Well"—Emarine laughed mirthfully—"she put the backs of her hands on her hips—this way!" She faced him suddenly, setting her arms akimbo, the shawl's fringes quivering over her elbows; her eyes fairly danced into his. "An' she looked at me a long time; then she says—'Hunh! *You —leetle—heifer!* You think you're some pun'kins, don't you? A-havin' a beau home from meetin'."

Both laughed hilariously.

"Well, what else 'id she say?"

"I don't believe you want to know. Do you —sure?"

"I cross my heart."

"Well — she said it c'u'dn't happen more'n ev'ry once 'n so often."

"Pshaw!"

"She did."

The young man paused abruptly. A narrow, unfrequented path led through deeper woods to the right.

"Emarine, let's take this catecornered cut through here."

"Oh, I'm afraid it's longer—an' it's washday, you know," said Emarine, with feeble resistance.

"We'll walk right fast. Come on. George! But it's nice and sweet in here, though!"

They entered the path. It was narrow and the great trees bent over and touched above them.

There was a kind of soft lavender twilight falling upon them. It was very still, save for the fluttering of invisible wings and the occasional shrill scream of a blue-jay.

"It *is* sweet in here," said Emarine.

The young man turned quickly, and with a deep, asking look into her lifted eyes, put his arms about her and drew her to him. "Emarine," he said, with passionate tenderness. And then he was silent, and just stood holding her crushed against him, and looking down on her with his very soul in his eyes. Oh, but a man who refrains from much speech in such an hour has wisdom straight from the gods themselves!

After a long silence Emarine lifted her head and smiled trustfully into his eyes. "It's washday," she said, with a flash of humor.

88

"So it is," he answered her, heartily. "An'
I promised yuh we'd hurry up—an' I alwus keep
my promises. But first—Emarine—"

"Well?"

"Yuh must say somethin' first."

"Say what, Mr. Parmer?"

"'Mr. Parmer!'" His tone and his look
were reproachful. "Can't choo say Orville?"

"Oh, I can—if you want I sh'u'd."

"Well, I do want choo sh'u'd, Emarine.
Now, yuh know what else it is I want choo
sh'u'd say before we go on."

"Why, no, I don't—hunh-unh." She shook
her head, coquettishly.

"Emarine"—the young fellow's face took on
a sudden seriousness—"I want choo to say yuh'll
marry me."

"Oh, my, no!" cried Emarine. She turned
her head on one side, like a bird, and looked at
him with lifted brows and surprised eyes. One
would have imagined that such a thought had
never entered that pretty head before.

"What, Emarine! Yuh won't?" There was
consternation in his voice.

"Oh, my, no!" Both glance and movement
were full of coquettishness. The very fringes of
the demure gray shawl seemed to have taken on
new life and vivacity.

Orville Palmer's face turned pale and stern.

He drew a long breath silently, not once removing that searching look from her face.

"Well, then," he said, calmly, "I want to know what choo mean by up an' lettin' me kiss yuh—if yuh don't mean to marry me."

This was an instant quietus to the girl's coquetry. She gave him a startled glance. A splash of scarlet came into each cheek. For a moment there was utter silence. Then she made a soft feint of withdrawing from his arms. To her evident amazement, he made no attempt to detain her. This placed her in an awkward dilemma, and she stood irresolutely, with her eyes cast down.

Young Palmer's arms fell at his sides with a movement of despair. Sometimes they were ungainly arms, but now absence of self-consciousness lent them a manly grace.

"Well, Emarine," he said, kindly, "I'll go back the way I come. Goodby."

With a quick, spontaneous burst of passion — against which she had been struggling, and which was girlish and innocent enough to carry a man's soul with it into heaven — Emarine cast herself upon his breast and flung her shawl-entangled arms about his shoulders. Her eyes were earnest and pleading, and there were tears of repentance in them. With a modesty that

was enchanting she set her warm, sweet lips
tremblingly to his, of her own free will.

"I didn't mean it," she whispered. "I was
only a — a-foolin'."

The year was older by a month when one
morning Mrs. Endey went to the front door and
stood with her body swaying backward, and one
rough hand roofing the rich light from her eyes.

"Emarine 'ad ought to 'a' got to the hill path
by this time," she said, in a grumbling tone.
"It beats me what keeps her so! I reckon she's
a-standin' like a bump on a lawg, watchin' a red
ant or a tumble-bug, or some fool thing! She'd
leave her dish-washin' any time an' stand at the
door a-ketchin' cold in her bare arms, with the
suds a-drippin' all over her apron an' the floor —
a-listenin' to one o' them silly meadow-larks
hollerin' the same noise over 'n over. Her paw's
women-folks are all just such fools."

She started guiltily and lowered her eyes to
the gate which had clicked sharply.

"Oh!" she said. "That you, Emarine?"
She laughed rather foolishly. "I was lookin'
right over you — lookin' *fer* you, too. Miss
Presly's be'n here, an' of all the strings she had
to tell! Why, fer pity's sake! Is that a dollar's
worth o' coffee?"

"Yes, it is; an' I guess it's full weight, too, from the way my arm feels! It's just about broke."

"Well, give it to me, an' come on out in the kitching. I've got somethin' to tell you."

Emarine followed slowly, pinning a spray of lilac bloom in her bosom as she went.

"Emarine, where's that spring balance at? I'm goin' to weigh this coffee. If it's one grain short, I'll send it back a-flyin'. I'll show 'em they can't cheat this old hen!"

She slipped the hook under the string and lifted the coffee cautiously until the balance was level with her eyes. Then standing well back on her heels and drawing funny little wrinkles up around her mouth and eyes, she studied the figures earnestly, counting the pounds and the half-pounds down from the top. Finally she lowered it with a disappointed air. "Well," she said, reluctantly, "it's just it — just to a 't.' They'd ought to make it a leetle over, though, to allow fer the paper bag. Get the coffee-canister, Emarine."

When the coffee had all been jiggled through a tin funnel into the canister, Mrs. Endey sat down stiffly and began polishing the funnel with a cloth. From time to time she glanced at Emarine with a kind of deprecatory mystery. At last she said — "Miss Presly spent the day down't Mis' Parmer's yesterday."

"Did she?" said Emarine, coldly; but the color came into her cheeks. "Shall I go on with the puddin'?"

"Why, you can if you want. She told me some things I don't like."

Emarine shattered an egg-shell on the side of a bowl and released the gold heart within.

"Miss Presly says once Mis' Parmer had to go out an' gether the eggs an' shet up the chickens, so Miss Presly didn't think there'd be any harm in just lookin' into the drawers an' things to see what she had. She says she's awful short on table cloths — only got three to her name! An' only six napkeens, an' them coarse 's anything! When Mis' Parmer come back in, Miss Presly talked around a little, then she says — 'I s'pose you're one o' them spic an' span kind, Mis' Parmer, that alwus has a lot o' extry table cloths put away in lavender.'"

Emarine set the egg-beater into the bowl and began turning it slowly.

"Mis' Parmer got mighty red all of a sudden; but she says right out — 'No, I'm a-gettin' reel short on table cloths an' things, Miss Presly, but I ain't goin' to replenish. Orville 's thinkin' o' gettin' married this year, an' I guess Emarine 'll have a lot o' extry things.' An' then she ups

93

an' laughs an' says — 'I'll let her stock up the house, seein's she's so anxious to get into it.' "

Emarine had turned pale. The egg-beater fairly flew round and round. A little of the golden foam slipped over the edge of the bowl and slid down to the white table.

"Miss Presly thinks a good deal o' you, Emarine, so that got her spunk up; an' she just told Mis' Parmer she didn't believe you was dyin' to go there an' stock up her drawers fer her. Says she — 'I don't think young people 'ad ought to live with mother-in-laws, any way.' Said she thought she'd let Mis' Parmer put that in her pipe an' smoke it when she got time."

There was a pulse in each side of Emarine's throat beating hard and full. Little blue, throbbing cords stood out in her temples. She went on mixing the pudding mechanically.

"Then Mis' Parmer just up an' said with a tantalizin' laugh that if you didn't like the a-commodations at her house, you needn't to come there. Said she never did like you, anyways, ner anybody else that set their heels down the way you set your'n. Said she'd had it all out with Orville, an' he'd promised her faithful that if there was any knucklin'-down to be done, you'd be the one to do it, an' not her!"

Emarine turned and looked at her mother. Her face was white with controlled passion. Her eyes burned. But her voice was quiet when she spoke.

"I guess you'd best move your chair," she said, "so 's I can get to the oven. This puddin' 's all ready to go in."

When she had put the pudding in the oven she moved about briskly, clearing the things off the table and washing them. She held her chin high. There was no doubt now about the click of her heels; it was ominous.

"I won't marry him!" she cried at last, flinging the words out. "He can have his mother an' his wore-out table cloths!" Her voice shook. The muscles around her mouth were twitching.

"My mercy!" cried her mother. She had a frightened look. "Who cares what his mother says? I w'u'dn't go to bitin' off my nose to spite my face, if I was you!"

"Well, I care what he says. I'll see myself knucklin'-down to a mother-in-law!"

"Well, now, don't go an' let loose of your temper, or you 'll be sorry fer it. You're alwus mighty ready a-tellin' me not to mind what folks say, an' to keep away from the old gossips."

"Well, you told me yourself, didn't you? I can't keep away from my own mother very well, can I?"

"Well, now, don't flare up so! You're worse 'n karosene with a match set to it."

"What 'id you tell me for, if you didn't want I sh'u'd flare up?"

"Why, I thought it 'u'd just put you on your mettle an' show her she c'u'dn't come it over you." Then she added, diplomatically changing her tone as well as the subject — "Oh, say, Emarine, I wish you'd go up in the antic an' bring down a bunch o' pennyrile. I'll watch the puddin'."

She laughed with dry humor when the girl was gone. "I got into a pickle that time. Who ever 'd 'a' thought she'd get stirred up so? I'll have to manage to get her cooled down before Orville comes to-night. They ain't many matches like him, if his mother *is* such an old scarecrow. He ain't so well off, but he'll humor Emarine up. He 'd lay down an' let her walk on him, I guess. There's Mis' Grisley b'en a-tryin' fer months to get him to go with her Lily — *Lily*, with a complexion like sole-leather! — an' a-askin' him up there all the time to dinner, an' a-flatterin' him up to the skies. I'd like to know what they always name dark-complected babies Lily fer! Oh, did you get the pennyrile, Emarine? I was laughin' to myself, a-wond'rin' what Mis' Grisley's Lily 'll say when she hears you're goin' to marry Orville."

Emarine hung a spotless dish-cloth on two nails behind the stove, but did not speak.

Mrs. Endey turned her back to the girl and smiled humorously.

"That didn't work," she thought. "I'll have to try somethin' else."

"I've made up my mind to get you a second-day dress, too, Emarine. You can have it any color you want — dove-color 'd be awful nice. There's a hat down at Mis' Norton's milliner' store that 'u'd go beautiful with dove-color."

Emarine took some flat-irons off the stove, wiped them carefully with a soft cloth and set them evenly on a shelf. Still she did not speak. Mrs. Endey's face took on an anxious look.

"There's some beautiful artaficial orange flowers at Mis' Norton's, Emarine. You can be married in 'em, if you want. They're so reel they almost smell sweet."

She waited a moment, but receiving no reply, she added with a kind of desperation — "An' a veil, Emarine — a long, white one a-flowin' down all over you to your feet — one that 'u'd just make Mis' Grisley's Lily's mouth water. What do you say to that? You can have that, too, if you want."

"Well, I don't want !" said Emarine, fiercely. "Didn't I say I wa'n't goin' to marry him ? I'll give him his walking-chalk when he comes to-night. I don't need any help about it, either."

She went out, closing the door as an exclamation point.

Oregon City kept early hours. The curfew ringing at nine o'clock on summer evenings gathered the tender-aged of both sexes off the street.

It was barely seven o'clock when Orville Palmer came to take Emarine out for a drive. He had a high top-buggy, rather the worse for wear, and drove a sad-eyed, sorrel horse.

She was usually ready to come tripping down the path, to save his tying the horse. To-night she did not come. He waited a while. Then he whistled and called — "Oh, Emarine!"

He pushed his hat back and leaned one elbow on his knee, flicking his whip up and down, and looking steadily at the open door. But she did not come. Finally he got out and, tying his horse, went up the path slowly. Through the door he could see Emarine sitting quietly sewing. He observed at once that she was pale.

"Sick, Emarine?" he said, going in.

"No," she answered, "I ain't sick."

"Then why under the sun didn't choo come when I hollowed?"

"I didn't want to." Her tone was icy.

He stared at her a full minute. Then he burst out laughing. "Oh, say, Emarine, yuh can be the contrariest girl I ever see! Yuh do love to tease a fellow so. Yuh'll have to kiss me fer that."

He went toward her. She pushed her chair

back and gave him a look that made him pause.

"How's your mother?" she asked.

"My mother?" A cold chill went up and down his spine. "Why — oh, she 's all right. Why?"

She took a small gold ring set with a circle of garnets from her finger and held it toward him with a steady hand.

"You can take an' show her this ring, an' tell her I ain't so awful anxious to stock her up on table cloths an' napkeens as she thinks I am. Tell her yuh 'll get some other girl to do her knucklin'-down fer her. I ain't that kind."

The young man's face grew scarlet and then paled off rapidly. He looked like a man accused of a crime. "Why, Emarine," he said, feebly.

He did not receive the ring, and she threw it on the floor at his feet. A whole month she had slept with that ring against her lips — the bond of her love and his! Now, it was only the emblem of her "knuckling-down" to another woman.

"You needn't to stand there a-pretendin' you don't know what I mean."

"Well, I don't, Emarine."

"Yes, you do, too. Didn't you promise your mother that if there was any knucklin'-down to be did, I'd be the one to do it, an' not her?"

"Why — er — Emarine —"

She laughed scornfully.

"Don't go to tryin' to get out of it. You know you did. Well, you can take your ring, an' your mother, an' all her old duds. I don't want any o' you."

"Emarine," said the young man, looking guilty and honest at the same time, "the talk I had with my mother didn't amount to a pinch o' snuff. It wa'n't anything to make yuh act this way. She don't like yuh just because I'm goin' to marry yuh"—

"Oh, but you ain't," interrupted Emarine, with an aggravating laugh.

"Yes, I am, too. She kep' naggin' at me day an' night fer fear yuh'd be sassy to her an' she'd have to take a back seat."

"I'll tell you what's the matter with her!" interrupted Emarine. "She's got the big-head. She thinks ev'ry body wants to rush into her old house, an' marry her son, an' use her old things! She wants to make ev'rybody toe *her* mark."

"Emarine! She's my mother."

"I don't care if she is. I w'u'dn't tech her with a ten-foot pole."

"She 'll be all r'ght after we're married, Emarine, an' she finds out how — how nice yuh are."

His own words appealed to his sense of the ridiculous. He smiled. Emarine divined the cause of his reluctant amusement and was instantly furious. Her face turned very white. Her eyes burned out of it like two fires.

"You think I ain't actin' very nice now, don't you? I don't care what you think, Orville Parmer, good or bad."

The young man stood thinking seriously.

"Emarine," he said, at last, very quietly, "I love yuh an' yuh know it. An' yuh love me. I'll alwus be good to yuh an' see that choo ain't emposed upon, Emarine. An' I think the world an' all of yuh. That's all I got to say. I can't see what ails yuh, Emarine. . . . . When I think o' that day when I asked yuh to marry me. . . . . An' that night I give yuh the ring"—the girl's eyelids quivered suddenly and fell. "An' that moonlight walk we took along by the falls. . . . . Why, it seems as if this can't be the same girl."

There was such a long silence that Mrs. Endey, cramping her back with one ear pressed to the keyhole of the door, decided that he had won and smiled dryly.

At last Emarine lifted her head. She looked at him steadily. "Did you, or didn't you, tell your mother I'd have to do the knucklin'-down?"

He shuffled his feet about a little.

"Well, I guess I did, Emarine, but I didn't mean anything. I just did it to get a little peace."

The poor fellow had floundered upon an unfortunate excuse.

"Oh !" said the girl, contemptuously. Her
lip curled. "An' so you come an' tell me the
same thing for the same reason — just to get a
little peace ! A pretty time you'd have a-gettin'
any peace at all, between the two of us ! You're
chickenish — an' I hate chickenish people."

" Emarine !"

"Oh, I wish you'd go." There was an almost
desperate weariness in her voice.

He picked up the ring with its shining garnet
stars, and went.

Mrs. Endey tiptoed into the kitchen.

"My back 's about broke." She laughed
noiselessly. "I swan I'm proud o' that girl.
She's got more o' me in her 'n I give her credit
fer. The idee o' her a-callin' him chickenish
right out to his face ! That done me good.
Well, I don't care such an awful lot if she don't
marry him. A girl with that much spunk deserves a *gov'nor* ! An' that mother o' his'n 's
a case. I guess her an' me 'd 'a' fit like cats an'
dogs, anyhow." Her lips unclosed with reluctant mirth.

The next morning Emarine arose and went
about her work as usual. She had not slept.
But there were no signs of relenting, or of regret,

in her face. After the first surreptitious look at her, Mrs. Endey concluded that it was all settled unchangeably. Her aspiring mind climbed from a governor to a United States senator. There was nothing impossible to a girl who could break her own heart at night and go about the next morning setting her heels down the way Emarine was setting hers.

Mrs. Endey's heart swelled with triumph.

Emarine washed the dishes and swept the kitchen. Then she went out to sweep the porch. Suddenly she paused. A storm of lyric passion had burst upon her ear ; and running through it she heard the words—"*Sweet — oh — Sweet · — my heart is breaking !*"

The girl trembled. Something stung her eyes sharply.

Then she pulled herself together stubbornly. Her face hardened. She went on sweeping with more determined care than usual.

"Well, I reckon," she said, with a kind of fierce philosophy, "it 'u'd 'a' been breaking a good sight worse if I'd 'a' married him an' that mother o' his'n. That's some comfort."

But when she went in she closed the door carefully, shutting out that impassioned voice.

PART II

It was eight o'clock of a June morning. It had rained during the night. Now the air was sweet with the sunshine on the wet leaves and flowers.

Mrs. Endey was ironing. The table stood across the open window, up which a wild honeysuckle climbed, flinging out slender, green shoots, each topped with a cluster of scarlet spikes. The splendor of the year was at its height. The flowers were marching by in pomp and magnificence.

Mrs. Endey spread a checked gingham apron on the ironing cloth. It was trimmed at the bottom with a ruffle, which she pulled and smoothed with careful fingers.

She selected an iron on the stove, set the wooden handle into it with a sharp, little click, and polished it on a piece of scorched newspaper. Then she moved it evenly across the starched apron. A shining path followed it.

At that moment some one opened the gate. Mrs. Endey stooped to peer through the vines.

"Well, 'f I ever 'n all my natcherl life!" she said, solemnly. She set the iron on its stand and lifted her figure erect. She placed one hand on her hip, and with the other rubbed her chin

in perplexed thought. "If it ain't Orville Parmer, you may shoot me! That beats me! I
wonder 'f he thinks Emarine 's a-dyin' o' love
fer him !"

Then a thought came that made her feel faint.
She fell into a chair, weakly. "Oh, my land !"
she said. "I wonder 'f that *ain't* what's the
matter of her ! I never'd thought o' that. I'd
thought o' ev'rything *but* that. I wonder !
There she's lied flat o' her back ever sence she
fell out with him a month ago. Oh, my mercy !
I wonder 'f that is it. Here I've b'en rackin'
my brains to find out what ails 'er."

She got up stiffly and went to the door. The
young man standing there had a pale, anxious
face.

"Good-mornin', Mis' Endey," he said. He
looked with a kind of entreaty into her grim
face. "I come to see Emarine."

"Emarine's sick." She spoke coldly.

"I know she is, Mis' Endey." His voice shook.
"If it wa'n't fer her bein' sick, I w'u'dn't be
here. I s'pose, after the way she sent me off, I
ain't got any spunk or I w'u'dn't 'a' come anyway ; but I heard—"

He hesitated and looked away.

"What 'id you hear ?"

"I heard she wa'n't a-goin' to—get well."

There was a long silence.

"Is she?" he asked, then. His voice was low and broken.

Mrs. Endey sat down. "I do' know," she said, after another silence. "I'm offul worried about her, Orville. I can't make out what ails 'er. She won't eat a thing; even floatin' island turns agi'n 'er — an' she al'ays loved that."

"Oh, Mis' Endey, can't I see 'er?"

"I don't see 's it 'u'd be any use. Emarine's turrable set. 'F you hadn't went an' told your mother that if there was any knucklin'-down to be did between her an' Emarine, Emarine 'u'd have to do it, you an' her'd 'a' b'en married by this time. I'd bought most ha'f her weddin' things a'ready."

The young man gave a sigh that was almost a groan. He looked like one whose sin has found him out. He dropped into a chair, and putting his elbows on his knees, sunk his face into his brown hands.

"Good God, Mis' Endey!" he said, with passionate bitterness. "Can't choo ever stop harpin' on that? Ain't I cursed myself day an' night ever sence? Oh, I wish yuh'd help me!" He lifted a wretched face. "I didn't mean any-thing by tellin' my mother that; she's a-gettin' kind o' childish, an' she was afraid Emarine 'u'd run over 'er. But if she'll only take me back, she'll have ev'rything her own way."

A little gleam of triumph came into Mrs. Endey's face. Evidently the young man was rapidly becoming reduced to a frame of mind desirable in a son-in-law.

"Will you promise that, solemn, Orville Parmer?" She looked at him sternly.

"Yes, Mis' Endey, I will — solemn." His tone was at once wretched and hopeful. "I'll promise anything under the sun, 'f she'll only fergive me. I can't *live* without 'er — an' that's all there is about it. Won't choo ask her to see me, Mis' Endey?"

"Well, I do' know," said Mrs. Endey, doubtfully. She cleared her throat, and sat looking at the floor, as if lost in thought. He should never have it to say that she had snapped him up too readily. "I don't feel much like meddlin'. I must say I side with Emarine. I do think"— her tone became regretful —"a girl o' her spir't deserves a gov'nor."

"I know she does," said the young man, miserably. "I alwus knew *I* wa'n't ha'f good enough fer 'er. But Mis' Endey, I know she loves me. Won't choo —"

"Well!" Mrs. Endey gave a sigh of resignation. She got up very slowly, as if still undecided. "I'll see what she says to 't. But I'll tell you right out I sha'n't advise 'er, Orville."

She closed the door behind her with deliberate

care. She laughed dryly as she went up stairs, holding her head high. "There's nothin' like makin' your own terms," she said, shrewdly.

She was gone a long time. When Orville heard her coming lumbering back down the stairs and along the hall, his heart stopped beating.

Her coming meant—everything to him; and it was so slow and so heavy it seemed ominous. For a moment he could not speak, and her face told him nothing. Then he faltered out—"Will she? Oh, don't choo say she won't!"

"Well," said Mrs. Endey, with a sepulchral sigh, "she'll see you, but I don't know 's anything 'll come of it. Don't you go to bracin' up on that idee, Orville Parmer. She's set like a strip o' calico washed in alum water."

The gleam of hope that her first words had brought to his face was transitory. "You can come on," said Mrs. Endey, lifting her chin solemnly.

Orville followed her in silence.

The little room in which Emarine lay ill was small and white, like a nun's chamber. The ceiling slanted on two sides. There was white matting on the floor; there was an oval blue rug of braided rags at the side of the bed, and another in front of the bureau. There was a small cane-seated and cane-backed rocker. By the side of the bed was a high, stiff wooden chair, painted very black and trimmed with very blue roses.

There were two or three pictures on the walls. The long curtains of snowy butter-cloth were looped high.

The narrow white bed had been wheeled across the open window, so Emarine could lie and look down over the miles of green valley, with the mellifluous Willamette winding through it like a broad silver-blue ribbon. By turning her head a little she could see the falls; the great bulk of water sliding over the precipice like glass, to be crushed into powdered foam and flung high into the sunlight, and then to go seething on down to the sea.

At sunrise and at sunset the mist blown up in long veils from the falls quickened of a sudden to rose and gold and purple, shifting and blending into a spectral glow of thrilling beauty. It was sweeter than guests to Emarine.

The robins were company, too, in the large cherry tree outside of her window; and sometimes a flight of wild canaries drifted past like a yellow, singing cloud. When they sank, swiftly and musically, she knew that it was to rest upon a spot golden with dandelions.

Outside the door of this room Mrs. Endey paused. "I don't see 's it 'u'd be proper to let you go in to see 'er alone," she said, sternly.

Orville's eyes were eloquent with entreaty. "Lord knows there w'u'dn't be any harm in 't," he said, humbly but fervently. "I feel jest as if I was goin' in to see an angel."

Mrs. Endey's face softened ; but at once a smile came upon it — one of those smiles of reluctant, uncontrollable humor that take us unawares sometimes, even in the most tragic moments. "She's got too much spunk fer an angel," she said.

"Don't choo go to runnin' of her down !" breathed Orville, with fierce and reckless defiance.

"I wa'n't a-runnin' of her down," retorted Mrs. Endey, coldly. "You don't ketch me a-runnin' of my own kin down, Orville Parmer !" She glowered at him under drawn brows. "An' I won't stand anybody else's a-runnin' of 'em down or a-walkin' over 'em, either ! There ain't no call fer *you* to tell me not to run 'em down." Her look grew blacker. "I reckon we'd best settle all about your mother before we go in there, Orville Parmer."

"What about 'er ?" His tone was miserable ; his defiance was short-lived.

"Why, there's no use 'n your goin' in there unless you're ready to promise that you'll give Emarine the whip-hand over your mother. You best make up your mind."

"It's *made* up," said the young fellow, desperately. "Lord Almighty, Mis' Endey, it's made up."

"Well." She turned the door-knob. "I know it ain't the thing, an' I'd die if Miss Presley sh'u'd come an' find out — the town w'u'dn't hold her, she'd talk so! Well! Now, don't stay too long. 'F I see anybody a-comin' I'll cough at the foot o' the stairs."

She opened the door and when he had passed in, closed it with a bitter reluctance. "It ain't the proper thing," she repeated; and she stood for some moments with her ear bent to the keyhole. A sudden vision of Miss Presley coming up the stairs to see Emarine sent her down to the kitchen with long, cautious strides, to keep guard.

Emarine was propped up with pillows. Her mother had dressed her in a white sacque, considering it a degree more proper than a nightdress. There was a wide ruffle at the throat, trimmed with serpentine edging. Emarine was famous for the rapidity with which she crocheted, as well as for the number and variety of her patterns.

Orville went with clumsy noiselessness to the white bed. He was holding his breath. His hungry eyes had a look of rising tears that are held back. They took in everything — the girl's paleness and her thinness; the beautiful dark hair, loose upon the pillow; the blue veins in her temples; the dark lines under her languid eyes.

He could not speak. He fell upon his knees, and threw one arm over her with compelling passion, but carefully, too, as one would touch a flower, and laid his brow against her hand. His shoulders swelled. A great sob struggled from his breast. "Oh, Emarine, Emarine!" he groaned. Then there was utter silence between them.

After a while, without lifting his head, he pushed her sleeve back a very little and pressed trembling, reverent lips upon the pulse beating irregularly in her slim wrist.

"Oh, Emarine!" he said, still without lifting his head. "I love yuh — I love yuh! I've suffered — oh, to think o' you layin' here sick, night after night fer a whole month, an' me not here to do things fer yuh. I've laid awake imaginin' that yuh wanted a fresh drink an' c'u'dn't make anybody hear; or that yuh wanted a cool cloth on your forrid, or a little jell-water, or somethin'. I've got up 'n the middle o' the night an' come an' stood out at your gate tell I'd see a shado' on the curt'n an' know yuh wa'n't alone. . . . . Oh, Emarine, Emarine!"

She moved her hand; it touched his throat and curved itself there, diffidently. He threw up his head and looked at her. A rush of passionate, startled joy stung through him like needles, filling his throat. He trembled strongly. Then his arms were about her and he had gathered her up against his breast; their lips were shaking together, after their long separation, in those kisses but one of which is worth a lifetime of all other kisses.

Presently he laid her back very gently upon her pillow, and still knelt looking at her with his hand on her brow. "I've tired yuh," he said, with earnest self-reproach. "I won't do 't ag'in, Emarine — I promise. When I looked 'n your eyes an' see that yuh'd fergive me; when I felt your hand slip 'round my neck, like it ust to, an' like I've b'en *starvin'* to feel it fer a month, Emarine — I c'u'dn't help it, nohow; but I won't do 't ag'in. Oh, to think that I've got choo back ag'in!"

He laid his head down, still keeping his arm thrown, lightly and tenderly as a mother's, over her.

The sick girl looked at him. Her face settled into a look of stubbornness; the exaltation that had transfigured it a moment before was gone. "You'll have to promise me," she said, "about your mother, you know. I'll have to be first."

"Yuh shall be, Emarine."

"You'll have to promise that if there's any knucklin'-down, she'll do 't, an' not me."

He moved uneasily. "Oh, don't choo worry, Emarine. It 'll be all right."

"Well, I want it settled now. You'll have to promise solemn that you'll stand by ev'rything I do, an' let me have things my way. If you don't, you can go back the way you come. But I know you'll keep your word if you promise."

"Yes," he said, "I will."

But he kept his head down and did not promise.

"Well?" she said, and faint as she was, her voice was like steel.

But still he did not promise.

After a moment she lifted her hand and curved it about his throat again. He started to draw away, but almost instantly shuddered closer to her and fell to kissing the white lace around her neck.

"Well," she said, coldly, "hurry an' make your choice. I hear mother a-comin'."

"Oh, Emarine!" he burst out, passionately. "I promise — I promise yuh ev'rything. My mother's gittin' old an' childish, an' it ain't right, but I can't give you up ag'in — I *can't!* I promise — I swear!"

Her face took on a tenderness worthy a nobler victory. She slipped her weak, bare arm up around him and drew his lips down to hers.

An hour later he walked away from the house,

114

the happiest man in Oregon City — or in all Oregon, for that matter. Mrs. Endey watched him through the vines. "Well, he's a-walkin' knee-deep in *promises*," she reflected, with a comfortable laugh, as 'she sent a hot iron hissing over a newly sprinkled towel. "I guess that mother o' his'n 'll learn a thing er two if she tries any o' her back-sass with Emarine."

Emarine gained strength rapidly. Orville urged an immediate marriage, but Mrs Endey objected. "I won't hear to 't tell Emarine gits her spunk back," she declared. "When she gits to settin' her heels down the way she ust to before she got sick, she can git married. I'll know then she's got her spunk back."

Toward the last of July Emarine commenced setting her heels down in the manner approved by her mother; so, on the first of August they were married and went to live with Mrs. Palmer. At the last moment Mrs. Endey whispered grimly — "Now, you mind you hold your head high."

"Hunh !" said Emarine. She lifted her chin so high and so suddenly that her long ear-rings sent out flashes in all directions.

They had been married a full month when Mrs. Endey went to spend a day at the Palmer's. She had a shrewd suspicion that all was not so tranquil there as it might be. She walked in unbidden and unannounced.

It was ten o'clock. The sun shown softly through the languid purple haze that brooded upon the valley. Crickets and grasshoppers crackled through the grasses and ferns. The noble mountains glimmered mistily in the distance.

Mrs. Palmer was sewing a patch on a tablecloth. Emarine was polishing silverware. "Oh !" she said, with a start. "You, is 't?"

"Yes," said Mrs. Endey, sitting down, "me. I come to spen' the day."

"I didn't hear yuh knock," said Mrs. Palmer, dryly. She was tall and stoop-shouldered. She had a thin, sour face and white hair. One knew, only to look at her, that life had given her all its bitters and but few of its sweets.

"I reckon not," said Mrs. Endey, "seein' I didn't knock. I don't knock at my own daughter's door. Well, forever ! Do you patch tablecloths, Mis' Parmer ? I never hear tell ! I have see darnt ones, but I never see a patched one." She laughed aggravatingly.

"Oh, that's nothin'," said Emarine, over her shoulder, "we have 'em made out o' flour sacks here, fer breakfas'."

Then Mrs. Palmer laughed — a thin, bitter laugh. Her face was crimson. "Yaas," she said, "I use patched table-cloths, an' table-cloths made out o' flour sacks; but I never did wear underclo's made out o' unbleached muslin in *my* life."

Then there was a silence. Emarine gave her mother a look, as much as to say — "What do you think of that?" Mrs. Endey smiled. "Thank mercy!" she said. "Dog-days 'll soon be over. The smoke's liftin' a leetle. I guess you an' Orville 'll git your house painted afore the fall rain comes on, Emarine? It needs it turrable bad."

"They ain't got the paintin' of it," said Mrs. Palmer, cutting a thread with her teeth. "It don't happen to be their house."

"Well, it's all the same. It 'll git painted if Emarine wants it sh'u'd. Oh, Emarine! Where'd you git them funny teaspoons at?"

"They're Orville's mother's." Emarine gave a mirthful titter.

"I want to know! Ain't them funny? Thin's no name fer 'm. You'd ought to see the ones my mother left me, Mis' Parmer — thick, my! One 'u'd make the whole dozen o' you'rn. I'll have 'em out an' ask you over to tea."

"I've heerd about 'em," said Mrs. Palmer, with the placidity of a momentary triumph. "The people your mother worked out fer give 'em to her, didn't they? My mother got her'n from her gran'mother. She never worked out.

She never lived in much style, but she al'ays had a plenty."

"My-*O!*" said Mrs. Endey, scornfully.

"I guess I'd best git the dinner on," said Emarine. She pushed the silver to one side with a clatter. She brought some green corn from the porch and commenced tearing off the pale emerald husks.

"D'you want I sh'u'd help shuck it?" said her mother.

"No; I'm ust to doin' 't alone."

A silence fell upon all three. The fire made a cheerful noise; the kettle steamed sociably; some soup-meat, boiling, gave out a savory odor. Mrs. Endey leaned back comfortably in her rocking-chair. There was a challenge in the very fold of her hands in her lap.

Mrs. Palmer sat erect, stiff and thin. The side of her face was toward Mrs. Endey. She never moved the fraction of an inch, but watched her hostilely out of the corner of her eye, like a hen on the defensive.

It was Mrs. Endey who finally renewed hostilities. "Emarine," she said, sternly, "what are you a-doin'? Shortenin' your biscuits with *lard?*"

"Yes."

Mrs. Endey sniffed contemptuously. "They won't be fit to eat! You feathered your nest,

didn't you? Fer mercy's sake! Can't you buy
butter to shorten your biscuits with? You'll be
makin' patata soup next!"

Then Mrs. Palmer stood up. There was a red
spot on each cheek.

"Mis' Endey," she said, "if yuh don't like
the 'comadations in this house, won't you be so
good 's to go where they're better? I must say
I never wear underclo's made out o' unbleached
muslin in *my* life! The hull town's see 'em on
your clo's line, an' tee-hee about it behind your
back. I notice your daughter was mighty
ready to git in here an 'shorten biscuits with lard,
an' use patched table-cloths, an'—"

"*Oh, mother!*"

It was her son's voice. He stood in the door.
His face was white and anxious. He looked at
the two women; then his eyes turned with a
terrified entreaty to Emarine's face. It was hard
as flint.

"It's time you come," she said, briefly.
"Your mother just ordered my mother out o'
doors. Whose house is this?"

He was silent.

"Say, Orville Parmer! whose house is this?"

"Oh, Emarine!"

"Don't you 'oh, Emarine' me! You answer
up!"

"Oh, Emarine, don't let's quar'l. We've only

119

b'en married a month. Let them quar'l, if they
want—"

"You answer up. Whose house is this?"

"It's mine," he said in his throat.

"You'rn! Your mother calls it her'n."

"Well, it is," he said, with a desperation that
rendered the situation tragic. "Oh, Emarine,
what's mine's her'n. Father left it to me, but o'
course he knew it 'u'd be her'n, too. She likes
to call it her'n."

"Well, she can't turn my mother out o' doors.
I'm your wife an' this is my house, if it's
you'rn. I guess it ain't hardly big enough fer
your mother an' me, too. I reckon one o' us had
best git out. I don't care much which, only I
don't knuckle-down to nobody. I won't be set
upon by nobody."

"Oh, Emarine!" There was terror in his
face and voice. He huddled into a chair and
covered his eyes with both hands. Mrs. Palmer,
also, sat down, as if her limbs had suddenly refused
to support her. Mrs. Endey ceased rocking and
sat with folded hands, grimly awaiting develop-
ments.

Emarine stood with the backs of her hands on
her hips. She had washed the flour off after putting the biscuits in the oven, and the palms were
pink and full of soft curves like rose leaves; her
thumbs were turned out at right angles. Her

cheeks were crimson, and her eyes were like diamonds.

"One o' us 'll have to git out," she said again.
"It's fer you to say which 'n, Orville Parmer.
I'd just as soon. I won't upbraid you, 'f you say
me."

"Well, I won't upbraid choo, if yuh say me,"
spoke up his mother. Her face was gray. Her
chin quivered, but her voice was firm. "Yuh
speak up, Orville."

Orville groaned—"Oh, mother! Oh, Emarine!"
His head sunk lower; his breast swelled with
great sobs—the dry, tearing sobs that in a man
are so terrible. "To think that you two women
sh'u'd both love me, an' then torcher me this
way! Oh, God, what can I do er say?"

Suddenly Emarine uttered a cry, and ran to
him. She tore his hands from his face and cast
herself upon his breast, and with her delicate
arms locked tight about his throat, set her warm,
throbbing lips upon his eyes, his brow, his mouth,
in deep, compelling kisses. "I'm your wife!
I'm your wife! I'm your wife!" she panted.
"You promised ev'rything to get me to marry
you! Can you turn me out now, an' make me a
laughin'-stawk fer the town? Can you give *me*
up? You love me, an' I love you! Let me show
you how I love you—"

She felt his arms close around her convulsively.

Then his mother arose and came to them, and
laid her wrinkled, shaking hand on his shoulder.
"My son," she said, "let *me* show yuh how *I*
love yuh. I'm your mother. I've worked fer
yuh, an' done fer yuh all your life, but the time's
come fer me to take a back seat. Its be'n hard —
it's be'n offul hard — an' I guess I've be'n mean
an' hateful to Emarine — but it's be'n hard.
Yuh keep Emarine, an' I'll go. Yuh want her
an' I want choo to be happy. Don't choo worry
about me — I'll git along all right. Yuh won't
have to decide — I'll go of myself. That's the
way *mothers* love, my son!"

She walked steadily out of the kitchen; and
though her head was shaking, it was carried
high.

PART III

It was the day before Christmas—an Oregon
Christmas. It had rained mistily at dawn; but
at ten o'clock the clouds had parted and moved
away reluctantly. There was a blue and dazzling
sky overhead. The rain-drops still sparkled on
the windows and on the green grass, and the last
roses and chrysanthemums hung their beautiful
heads heavily beneath them; but there was to be
no more rain. Oregon City's mighty barometer—
the Falls of the Willamette—was declaring to her

people by her softened roar that the morrow was to be fair.

Mrs. Orville Palmer was in the large kitchen making preparations for the Christmas dinner. She was a picture of dainty loveliness in a lavender gingham dress, made with a full skirt and a shirred waist and big leg-o'-mutton sleeves. A white apron was tied neatly around her waist.

Her husband came in, and paused to put his arm around her and kiss her. She was stirring something on the stove, holding her dress aside with one hand.

"It's goin' to be a fine Christmas, Emarine," he said, and sighed unconsciously. There was a wistful and careworn look on his face.

"Beautiful!" said Emarine, vivaciously. "Goin' down-town, Orville?"

"Yes. Want anything?"

"Why, the cranberries ain't come yet. I'm so uneasy about 'em. They'd ought to 'a' b'en stooed long ago. I like 'em cooked down an' strained to a jell. I don't see what ails them groc'rymen! Sh'u'd think they c'u'd get around some time before doomsday! Then, I want—here, you'd best set it down." She took a pencil and a slip of paper from a shelf over the table and gave them to him. "Now, let me see." She commenced stirring again, with two little wrinkles between her brows. "A ha'f a pound o' citron; a

ha'f a pound o' candied peel; two pounds o'
cur'nts; two pounds o' raisins—git 'em stunned,
Orville; a pound o' sooet—make 'em give you
some that ain't all strings! A box o' Norther'
Spy apples; a ha'f a dozen lemons; four-bits'
worth o' walnuts or a'monds, whichever's fresh-
est; a pint o' Puget Sound oysters fer the dressin',
an' a bunch o' cel'ry. You stop by an' see about
the turkey, Orville; an' I wish you'd run in 's
you go by mother's an' tell her to come up as
soon as she can. She'd ought to be here now."

Her husband smiled as he finished the list.
"You're a wonderful housekeeper, Emarine," he
said.

Then his face grew grave. "Got a present fer
your mother yet, Emarine?"

"Oh, yes, long ago. I got 'er a black shawl
down t' Charman's. She's b'en wantin' one."

He shuffled his feet about a little. "Unh-
hunh. Yuh—that is—I reckon yuh ain't picked
out any present fer—fer my mother, have yuh,
Emarine?"

"No," she replied, with cold distinctness. "I
ain't."

There was a silence. Emarine stirred briskly.
The lines grew deeper between her brows. Two
red spots came into her cheeks. "I hope the rain
ain't spoilt the chrysanthums," she said then,
with an air of ridding herself of a disagreeable
subject.

124

Orville made no answer. He moved his feet again uneasily. Presently he said: "I expect my mother needs a black shawl, too. Seemed to me her'n looked kind o' rusty at church Sunday. Notice it, Emarine?"

"No," said Emarine.

"Seemed to me she was gittin' to look offul old. Emarine"—his voice broke; he came a step nearer—"it'll be the first Christmas dinner I ever eat without my mother."

She drew back and looked at him. He knew the look that flashed into her eyes, and shrank from it.

"You don't have to eat this 'n' without 'er, Orville Parmer! You go an' eat your dinner with your mother, 'f you want! I can get along alone. Are you goin' to order them things? If you ain't, just say so, an' I'll go an' do 't myself!"

He put on his hat and went without a word.

Mrs. Palmer took the saucepan from the stove and set it on the hearth. Then she sat down and leaned her cheek in the palm of her hand, and looked steadily out of the window. Her eyelids trembled closer together. Her eyes held a far-sighted look. She saw a picture; but it was not the picture of the blue reaches of sky, and the green valley cleft by its silver-blue river. She saw a kitchen, shabby, compared to her own,

125

scantily furnished, and in it an old, white-haired woman sitting down to eat her Christmas dinner alone.

After a while she arose with an impatient sigh. "Well, I can't help it!" she exclaimed. "If I knuckled-down to her this time, I'd have to do 't ag'in. She might just as well get ust to 't, first as last. I wish she hadn't got to lookin' so old an' pitiful, though, a-settin' there in front o' us in church Sunday after Sunday. The cords stand out in her neck like well-rope, an' her chin keeps a-quiv'rin' so! I can see Orville a-watch-in' her——"

The door opened suddenly and her mother entered. She was bristling with curiosity. "Say, Emarine!" She lowered her voice, although there was no one to hear. "Where d' you s'pose the undertaker's a-goin' up by here? Have you hear of anybody——"

"No," said Emarine. "Did Orville stop by an' tell you to hurry up?"

"Yes. What's the matter of him? Is he sick?"

"Not as I know of. Why?"

"He looks so. Oh, I wonder if it's one o' the Peterson childern where the undertaker's a-goin'! They've all got the quinsy sore throat."

"How does he look? I don't see 's he looks so turrable."

"Why, Emarine Parmer! Ev'rybody in town says he looks *so!* I only hope they don't know what ails him!"

"What *does* ail him?" cried out Emarine, fiercely. "What are you hintin' at?"

"Well, if you don't know what ails him, you'd ort to; so I'll tell you. He's dyin' by inches ever sence you turned his mother out o' doors."

Emarine turned white. Sheet lightning played in her eyes.

"Oh, you'd ought to talk about my turnin' her out!" she burst out, furiously. "After you a-settin' here a-quar'l'n' with her in this very kitchen, an' eggin' me on! Wa'n't she goin' to turn you out o' your own daughter's home? Wa'n't that what I turned her out fer? I didn't turn her out, anyhow! I only told Orville this house wa'n't big enough fer his mother an' me, an' that neither o' us 'u'd knuckle-down, so he'd best take his choice. You'd ought to talk!"

"Well, if I egged you on, I'm sorry fer 't," said Mrs. Endey, solemnly. "Ever sence that fit o' sickness I had a month ago, I've feel kind o' old an' no account myself, as if I'd like to let all holts go, an' just rest. I don't spunk up like I ust to. No, he didn't go to Peterson's—he's gawn right on. My land! I wonder 'f it ain't old gran'ma Eliot; she had a bad spell—no, he didn't turn that corner. I can't think where he's goin' to!"

She sat down with a sigh of defeat.

A smile glimmered palely across Emarine's face and was gone. "Maybe if you'd go up in the antic you could see better," she suggested, dryly.

"Oh, Emarine, here comes old gran'ma Eliot herself! Run an' open the door fer 'er. She's limpin' worse 'n usual."

Emarine flew to the door. Grandma Eliot was one of the few people she loved. She was large and motherly. She wore a black dress and shawl and a funny bonnet, with a frill of white lace around her brow.

Emarine's face softened when she kissed her. "I'm so glad to see you," she said, and her voice was tender.

Even Mrs. Endey's face underwent a change. Usually it wore a look of doubt, if not of positive suspicion, but now it fairly beamed. She shook hands cordially with the guest and led her to a comfortable chair.

"I know your rheumatiz is worse," she said, cheerfully, "because you're limpin' so. Oh, did you see the undertaker go up by here? We can't think where he's goin' to. D' you happen to know?"

"No, I don't; an' I don't want to, neither."

Mrs. Eliot laughed comfortably. "Mis' Endey, you don't ketch me foolin' with undertakers till I have to." She sat down and removed her black cotton gloves. "I'm gettin' to that age when I don't care much where undertakers go to so long 's they let *me* alone. Fixin' fer Christmas dinner, Emarine dear?"

"Yes, ma'am," said Emarine in her very gentlest tone. Her mother had never said "dear" to her, and the sound of it on this old lady's lips was sweet. "Won't you come an' take dinner with us?"

The old lady laughed merrily. "Oh, dearie me, dearie me! You don't guess my son's folks could spare me now, do you? I spend ev'ry Christmas there. They most carry me on two chips. My son's wife, Sidonie, she nearly runs her feet off waitin' on me. She can't do enough fer me. My, Mrs. Endey, you don't know what a comfort a daughter-in-law is when you get old an' feeble!"

Emarine's face turned red. She went to the table and stood with her back to the older woman; but her mother's sharp eyes observed that her ears grew scarlet.

"An' I never will," said Mrs. Endey, grimly. "You've got a son-in-law, though, who's worth a whole townful of most son-in-laws. He was such a good son, too; jest worshipped his mother;

couldn't bear her out o' his sight. He humored her high an' low. That's jest the way Sidonie does with me. I'm gettin' cranky 's I get older, an' sometimes I'm reel cross an' sassy to her; but she jest laffs at me, an' then comes an' kisses me, an' I'm all right ag'in. It's a blessin' right from God to have a daughter-in-law like that.''

The knife in Emarine's hand slipped, and she uttered a little cry.

"Hurt you?" demanded her mother, sternly.

Emarine was silent, and did not turn.

"Cut you, Emarine? Why don't you answer me? Aigh?''

"A little," said Emarine. She went into the pantry, and presently returned with a narrow strip of muslin which she wound around her finger.

"Well, I never see! You never will learn any gumption! Why don't you look what you're about? Now, go around Christmas with your finger all tied up!''

"Oh, that'll be all right by to-morrow," said Mrs. Eliot, cheerfully. "Won't it, Emarine? Never cry over spilt milk, Mrs. Endey; it makes a body get wrinkles too fast. O' course Orville's mother's comin' to take dinner with you, Emarine.''

"Dear me!" exclaimed Emarine, in a sudden flutter. "I don't see why them cranberries don't come! I told Orville to hurry 'em up. I'd best make the floatin' island while I wait."

"I stopped at Orville's mother's as I came along."

"How?" Emarine turned in a startled way from the table.

"I say, I stopped at Orville's mother's as I come along, Emarine."

"Oh!"

"She well?" asked Mrs. Endey.

"No, she ain't; shakin' like she had the Saint Vitus dance. She's failed harrable lately. She'd b'en cryin'; her eyes was all swelled up."

There was quite a silence. Then Mrs. Endey said—"What she b'en cryin' about?"

"Why, when I asked her she jest laffed kind o' pitiful, an' said: 'Oh, only my tomfoolishness, o' course.' Said she always got to thinkin' about other Christmases. But I cheered her up. I told her what a good time I always had at my son's, and how Sidonie jest couldn't do enough fer me. An' I told her to think what a nice time she'd have here 't Emarine's to-morrow."

Mrs. Endey smiled. "What she say to that?"

"She didn't say much. I could see she was thankful, though, she had a son's to go to. She said she pitied all poor wretches that had to set out their Christmas alone. Poor old lady! she ain't got much spunk left. She's all broke down.

But I cheered her up some. Sech a *wishful* look took holt o' her when I pictchered her dinner over here at Emarine's. I can't seem to forget it. Goodness! I must go. I'm on my way to Sidonie's, an' she'll be comin' after me if I ain't on time."

When Mrs. Eliot had gone limping down the path, Mrs. Endey said: "You got your front room red up, Emarine?"

"No; I ain't had time to red up anything."

"Well, I'll do it. Where's your duster at?"

"Behind the org'n. You can get out the wax cross again. Mis' Dillon was here with all her childern, an' I had to hide up ev'rything. I never see childern like her'n. She lets 'em handle things so!"

Mrs. Endey went into the "front room" and began to dust the organ. She was something of a diplomat, and she wished to be alone for a few minutes. "You have to manage Emarine by contrairies," she reflected. It did not occur to her that this was a family trait. "I'm offul sorry I ever egged her on to turnin' Orville's mother out o' doors, but who'd 'a' thought it 'u'd break her down so? She ain't told a soul either. I reckoned she'd talk somethin' offul about us, but she ain't told a soul. She's kep' a stiff upper lip an' told folks she al'ays expected to live alone when Orville got married. Emarine's all worked up.

132

I believe the Lord hisself must 'a' sent gran'ma Eliot here to talk like an angel unawares. I bet she'd go an' ask Mis' Parmer over here to dinner if she wa'n't afraid I'd laff at her fer knucklin'-down. I'll have to aggravate her."

She finished dusting, and returned to the kitchen. "I wonder what gran'ma Eliot 'u'd say if she knew you'd turned Orville's mother out, Emarine?"

There was no reply. Emarine was at the table mixing the plum pudding. Her back was to her mother.

"I didn't mean what I said about bein' sorry I egged you on, Emarine. I'm glad you turned her out. She'd *ort* to be turned out."

Emarine put a handful of floured raisins into the mixture and stirred it all together briskly.

"Gran'ma Eliot can go talkin' about her daughter-in-law Sidonie all she wants, Emarine. You keep a stiff upper lip."

"I can 'tend to my own affairs," said Emarine, fiercely.

"Well, don't flare up so. Here comes Orville. Land, but he does look peakid !"

After supper, when her mother had gone home for the night, Emarine put on her hat and shawl.

Her husband was sitting by the fireplace, looking thoughtfully at the bed of coals.

"I'm goin' out," she said, briefly. "You keep the fire up."

"Why, Emarine, its dark. Don't choo want I sh'u'd go along?"

"No; you keep the fire up."

He looked at her anxiously, but he knew from the way she set her heels down that remonstrance would be useless.

"Don't stay long," he said, in a tone of habitual tenderness. He loved her passionately, in spite of the lasting hurt she had given him when she parted him from his mother. It was a hurt that had sunk deeper than even he realized. It lay heavy on his heart day and night. It took the blue out of the sky, and the green out of the grass, and the gold out of the sunlight; it took the exaltation and the rapture out of his tenderest moments of love.

He never reproached her, he never really blamed her; certainly he never pitied himself. But he carried a heavy heart around with him, and his few smiles were joyless things.

For the trouble he blamed only himself. He had promised Emarine solemnly before he married her that if there were any "knuckling-down" to be done, his mother should be the one to do it. He had made the promise deliberately, and he could no more have broken it than he could have changed the color of his eyes. When bitter

134

feeling arises between two relatives by marriage, it is the one who stands between them — the one who is bound by the tenderest ties to both — who has the real suffering to bear, who is torn and tortured until life holds nothing worth the having.

Orville Palmer was the one who stood between. He had built his own cross, and he took it up and bore it without a word.

Emarine hurried through the early winter dark until she came to the small and poor house where her husband's mother lived. It was off the main-traveled street.

There was a dim light in the kitchen ; the curtain had not been drawn. Emarine paused and looked in. The sash was lifted six inches, for the night was warm, and the sound of voices came to her at once. Mrs. Palmer had company.

"It's Miss Presly," said Emarine, resentfully, under her breath. "Old gossip !"

" — goin' to have a fine dinner, I hear," Miss Presly was saying. "Turkey with oyster dressin', an' cranberries, an' mince an' pun'kin pie, an' reel plum puddin' with brandy poured over 't an' set afire, an' wine dip, an' nuts, an' raisins, an' wine itself to wind up on. Emarine's a fine cook. She knows how to get up a dinner that makes your mouth water to think about. You goin' to have a spread, Mis' Parmer ?"

135

"Not much of a one," said Orville's mother. "I expected to, but I c'u'dn't get them fall patatas sold off. I'll have to keep 'em till spring to git any kind o' price. I don't care much about Christmas, though " — her chin was trembling, but she lifted it high. "It's silly for anybody but childern to build so much on Christmas."

Emarine opened the door and walked in. Mrs. Palmer arose slowly, grasping the back of her chair. "Orville's dead?" she said, solemnly.

Emarine laughed, but there was the tenderness of near tears in her voice. "Oh, my, no!" she said, sitting down. "I run over to ask you to come to Christmas dinner. I was too busy all day to come sooner. I'm goin' to have a great dinner, an' I've cooked ev'ry single thing of it myself! I want to show you what a fine Christmas dinner your daughter-'n-law can get up. Dinner's at two, an' I want you to come at eleven. Will you?"

Mrs. Palmer had sat down, weakly. Trembling was not the word to describe the feeling that had taken possession of her. She was shivering. She wanted to fall down on her knees and put her arms around her son's wife, and sob out all her loneliness and heartache. But life is a stage; and Miss Presly was an audience not to be ignored. So Mrs. Palmer said : "Well, I'll be reel glad o come, Emarine. It's offul kind o' yuh to think of 't. It 'u'd 'a' be'n lonesome eatin' here all by myself, I expect.''

Emarine stood up. Her heart was like a this-tle-down. Her eyes were shining. "All right," she said ; "an' I want that you sh'u'd come just at eleven. I must run right back now. Good-night."

"Well, I declare!" said Miss Presly. "That girl gits prettier ev'ry day o' her life. Why, she just looked full o' *glame* to-night!"

Orville was not at home when his mother ar-rived in her rusty best dress and shawl. Mrs. Endey saw her coming. She gasped out, "Why, good grieve! Here's Mis' Parmer, Emarine!"

"Yes, I know," said Emarine, calmly. "I ast her to dinner."

She opened the door, and shook hands with her mother-in-law, giving her mother a look of de-fiance that almost upset that lady's gravity.

"You set right down, Mother Parmer, an' let me take your things. Orville don't know you're comin', an' I just want to see his face when he comes in. Here's a new black shawl fer your Christmas. I got mother one just like it. See what nice long fringe it's got. Oh, my, don't go to cryin'! Here comes Orville."

She stepped aside quickly. When her husband

137

entered his eyes fell instantly on his mother, weeping childishly over the new shawl. She was in the old splint rocking-chair with the high back. "*Mother!*" he cried ; then he gave a frightened, tortured glance at his wife. Emarine smiled at him, but it was through tears.

"Emarine ast me, Orville — she ast me to dinner o' herself! An' she give me this shawl. I'm — cryin' — fer — joy———"

"I ast her to dinner," said Emarine, "but she ain't ever goin' back again. She's goin' to *stay*. I expect we've both had enough of a lesson to do us."

Orville did not speak. He fell on his knees and laid his head, like a boy, in his mother's lap, and reached one strong but trembling arm up to his wife's waist, drawing her down to him.

Mrs. Endey got up and went to rattling things around on the table vigorously. "Well, I never see sech a pack o' loonatics!" she exclaimed. "Go an' burn all your Christmas dinner up, if I don't look after it! Turncoats! I expect they'll both be fallin' over theirselves to knuckle-down to each other from now on! I never see!"

But there was something in her eyes, too, that made them beautiful.

THE CUTTIN'-OUT OF BART WINN

THE CUTTIN'-OUT OF BART WINN

"Lavin-ee !"

"Well ?"

Mrs. Vaiden came to the foot of the stairs.

"You up there ?" she said.

"Yes, maw. What you want ?"

"Somebody's comin'," said Mrs. Vaiden, lowering her voice to a tone of important mystery.

"I guess not here," said Lavinia, lightly. She sat down on the top step and smiled at her mother.

"Yes, it is here, too," retorted Mrs. Vaiden, with some irritation. "If you couldn't conterdict a body 't wouldn't be you ! You're just like your paw !" She paused, and then added : "It's a man a-foot. He's comin' up the path slow, a-stoppin' to look at the flowers."

"Maybe it's the minister," said the girl, still regarding her mother with a good-natured, teasing smile.

"No, it ain't the minister, either. As if I didn't know the minister when I see him ! You do aggravate me so ! It's a young fello', an' he's all dressed up. You'll have to go to the door."

"Oh, maw !" cried Lavinia, reproachfully. "I just can't ! In this short dress ?"

141

She stood up, with a look of dismay, and began pulling nervously at her fresh gingham skirt. It was short, showing very prettily-arched insteps and delicate ankles.

"Well, you just can, an' haf to," said Mrs. Vaiden, shortly. "I've told you often enough to put a ruffle on the bottom o' that dress, an' I'm glad you're caught. Mebbe you'll do's I tell you after this —"

She started guiltily as a loud rap sounded upon the door behind her, and began to tiptoe heavily down the hall toward the kitchen. The girl looked after her in mingled amusement and chagrin. Then she leaned forward slightly, drawing the skirt back closely on both sides, and looked at her feet, with her head turned on one side like a bird. When the cessation of her mother's labored breathing announced silently that she had reached the kitchen in safety, Lavinia shrugged her beautiful shoulders — which no gown could conceal — and opened the door. A young man in a light traveling-suit stood before her. In his hand was a bunch of her own sweet-peas.

At sight of her he whisked off his hat in a way that brought a lovely color to her face and throat. For a little while it seemed as if he were not going to say or do anything but just look at her. She was well worth looking at. She had the rare beauty of velvet eyes of a reddish-brown color, hair wavy and brown, with red glints in it, and a clear complexion, unfreckled and of exquisite coloring.

Lavinia's eyes went to the sweet-peas, and then, with a deeper blush under them, to his face.

"Won't you come in?" she said.

"Why, yes, if you'll let me." The young man smiled, and Lavinia found her lips and eyes responding, in all the lightness of youth and a clear conscience.

"I couldn't help taking some of your sweet-peas," he said, following her into the parlor. It was a large, solemn-looking room. The blinds were lowered over the windows, but the girl raised one slightly, letting a splash of pale autumnal sunshine flicker across the hit-and-miss rag carpet. There was an organ in one corner and a hair-cloth sofa in another. Eight slender-legged hair-cloth chairs were placed at severely equal distances around the room, their backs resting firmly against the walls. All tipped forward slightly, their front legs being somewhat shorter than the others. On the back of each was a small, square crocheted tidy. There were some family portraits on the walls, in oval gilt frames; and there was a large picture of George Washington and family, on their stateliest behavior; another, named in large letters "The Journey of Life," of an uncommonly roomy row-boat con-

taining at least a dozen persons, who were supposed to represent all ages from the cradle to
the grave; in the wide, white margin beneath
this picture were two verses of beautiful, des-
criptive poetry, and in one corner appeared, with
apparent irrelevancy, the name of an illustrated
newspaper. There was also a chromo of a scantily-
attired woman clinging to a cross which was set
in the midst of dashing sea-waves; and there
was a cheerful photograph, in a black cloth frame,
of flowers — made into harps, crosses, anchors
and hearts — which had been sent at some time
of bereavement by sympathetic but misguided
friends. A marble-topped centre-table held a
large plush album, a scrap book, a book of
autographs, a lamp with a pale-green shade, and
a glass case containing a feather-wreath.

"Oh, we've got lots of sweet-peas," said
Lavinia, adjusting the blind carefully. Then she
looked at him.

"May I see Mrs. Vaiden?" he asked, easily.

"She's — busy," said Lavinia, with a look of
embarrassment. "But I'll see —"

"Oh, don't," interrupted the young man
lightly. "They told me at the post-office she took
boarders sometimes, and I came to see if there
was a chance for me." He handed a card to the
girl with an air of not knowing that he was doing
it. Her very eyelids seemed to blush as she looked

at it and read the name — Mr. C. Daun Diller.
"I am writing up the Puget Sound country for a
New York paper, and I should like to make my
headquarters here at Whatcom, but I can't stand
the hotels in your new towns. It's the most amaz-
ing thing!" he went on, smiling at her as she
stood twisting the card in her fingers, not knowing exactly what to do with it. "You go to
sleep at night in a Puget Sound village with the
fronts of the stores painted green, blue and red,
spasmodic patches of sidewalk here and there,
dust ankle deep, and no street-lights — and you
wake in the morning in a *city!* A city with fine
stone blocks and residences, stone pavements,
electric lights and railways, gas, splendid water-
works,"—he was checking off now, excitedly, on
his fingers,—"sewerage, big mills, factories, can-
neries, public schools that would make the East
stare, churches, libraries"—he stopped abruptly,
and, dropping his arms limply to his sides, added
—"and not a hotel! Not a comfortable bed or
a good meal to be had for love or money!"

"Yes, that's so," said Lavinia, reluctantly.
"But you can't expect us to get everything all
at onct. Why, Whatcom's boom only started
in six months ago."

Mr. C. Daun Diller looked amused. "Oh, if
it were this town only," he said, sitting down on
one of the hair cloth chairs and feeling himself

slide gently forward, "I shouldn't have mentioned it. But the truth is, there are only three decent hotels in the whole Puget Sound country. But I know"—here he smiled at her again—"that it's not safe to breathe a word against Puget Sound to a Puget-Sounder."

"No, it ain't," said the girl, responding to the smile and the respectfully bantering tone. Then she moved to the door. "Well, I'll see what maw says to it," she said, and vanished.

Mr. C. Daun Diller stood up and pushed his hands down into his pockets, whistling softly. He walked over to the organ and looked at the music. There were three large books: "The Home Circle," "The Golden Chord," and "The Family Treasure;" a "simplified" copy of "The Maiden's Prayer," and a book of "Gospel Songs."

The young man smiled.

"All the same," he said, as if in answer to a disparaging remark made by some one else, "she's about the handsomest girl I ever saw. I'm getting right down anxious to see myself what 'maw' will 'say to it.'"

After a long while Mrs. Vaiden appeared in a crisply-starched gingham dress and a company manner—both of which had been freshly put on for the occasion. Mr. Diller found her rather painfully polite, and he began to wonder, after paying his first week's board, whether he could endure two or three months of her; but he was quite, quite sure that he could endure a full year of the daughter.

A couple of evenings later he was sitting by the window in his quaint but exquisitely neat room, writing, when a light rap came upon his door. Upon opening it he found Lavinia standing, bashfully, a few steps away. There was a picturesque, broad-brimmed hat set coquettishly on her splendid hair.

"Maw wanted I sh'u'd ask you if you'd like to see an Indian canoe-race," she said.

"*Would* I?" he ejaculated, getting into a great excitement at once. "Well, I should say so! Awfully good of your mother to think—but where is it—when is it? How can I see it?"

"It's down by the viaduck—right now," said Lavinia. Then she added, shyly, pretending to be deeply engrossed with her glove: "I'm just goin'."

"Oh, are you?" said Diller, seizing his hat and stick and coming eagerly out to her. "And may I go with you? Will you take me in hand? I haven't the ghost of an idea where the viaduct is."

"Oh, yes, I'll show you," she said, with a glad little laugh, and they went swiftly down the stairs and out into the sweet evening.

"You know," she said, as he opened the gate for her with a deference to which she was not accustomed, and which gave her a thrill of innocent exultation, "the Alaska Indians are just comin' back from hop-pickin' down around Puyallup an' Yakima an' Seattle, an' they alwus stop here an' have races with the Lummies an' the Nooksacks."

Mr. Diller drew a deep breath.

"Do you know," he said, "I wouldn't have missed this for anything—not for anything I can think of. And yet I should if it hadn't been for "—he hesitated, and then added—"your mother." They looked into each other's eyes and laughed, very foolishly and happily.

The sun was setting—moving slowly, scarlet and of dazzling brilliancy, down the western sky, which shaded rapidly from pale blue to salmon, and from salmon to palest pea-green. Beneath, superbly motionless, at full tide, the sound stretched mile on mile away to Lummi peninsula, whose hills the sun now touched—every fir-tree on those noble crests standing out against that burnished background. A broad, unbroken path of gold stretched from shore to shore. Some sea-gulls were circling in endless, silvery rings through the amethystine haze between sea and sky. The old, rotten pier running a mile out to sea shone like a strip of gold above the deep blue water. It was crowded with people, indifferent to danger in their eagerness to see the races. Indeed, there seemed to be people everywhere ; on the high banks, the piers, and the mills scattered over the tide-flats, and out in row boats. Two brass bands were playing stirring strains alternately. There was much excitement—much shouting, hurrying, running. The crowd kept swaying from the viaduct over to the pier, and from the pier back to the viaduct. Nobody seemed to be quite sure where the start would be ; even the three judges, when asked, yelled back, as they clambered down to their row-boat : " We don't know. Wait and see ! "

" What accommodating persons," said Mr. Diller, cheerfully. " Shall we go over to the pier ? The tide seems to be running that way."

" Oh, the tide's not running now," said Lavinia. " It's full."

Diller looked amused. " I meant the people," he said.

The girl laughed and looked around on the pushing crowd. " I guess we'd best stop right here on the viaduck ; here's just where they started last year an' the year before. Oh, see, here's the Alaskas camped pretty near under us !"

As she lifted her voice a little Diller saw a young man standing near start and turn toward her with a glad look of recognition ; but at once his glance rested on Diller, and his expression changed to a kind of puzzled bewilderment. The girl was leaning over the railing and did not see him, but he never took his eyes away from her and Diller.

There was a long wait, but the crowd did not lose its patience or its good humor. There was considerable betting going on, and there was the same exciting uncertainty about the start. The sun went down and a bank of apricot-colored clouds piled low over the snow crest of Mount Baker in the East. The pier darkened and the path of gold faded, but splashes of scarlet still lingered on the blue water. A chill, sweet wind started up suddenly, and some of the girl's bronze curls got loose about her white temples. Diller put her wrap around her carefully, and she smiled up at him deliciously. Then she cried out. "Oh, they're gettin' into the boat! They're goin' to start. Oh, I'm so glad!" and struck her two hands together gleefully, like a child.

The long, narrow, richly-painted and carven canoe slid down gracefully into the water. Eleven tall, supple Alaskan Indians, bare to the waist, leaped lightly to their places. They sat erect, close to the sides of the boat, holding their short paddles perpendicularly. At a signal the paddles shot straight down into the water, and, with a swift, magnificent straining and swelling of muscles in the powerful bronze arms and bodies, were pushed backward and withdrawn in lightning strokes. The canoe flashed under the viaduct and appeared on the other side, and a great shout belched from thousands of throats. From camping-places farther up the shore the other boats darted out into the water and headed for the viaduct.

"Oh, good! good!" cried Lavinia in a very ecstasy of excitement. "They're goin' to start right under us. We're just in *the* place!"

"Twenty dollars on the Nooksacks!" yelled a blear-eyed man in a carriage. "Twenty! Twenty ag'inst ten on the Nooksacks!"

The band burst into "Hail, Columbia!" with beautiful irrelevancy. The crowd came surging back from the pier. Diller was excited, too. His face was flushed and he was breathing heavily. "Who'll you bet on?" he asked, laughing, and thinking, even at that moment, how ravishingly lovely she was with that glow on her face and the loose curls blowing about her face and throat.

"Oh, the *Alaskas!*" cried the girl, striking little blows of impatience on the railing with her soft fists. "They're so tall an' fine-lookin'! They're so strong an' grand! Look at their muscles—just like ropes! Oh, I'll bet on the Alaskas! I *love* tall men!"

"Do you?" said Diller. "I'm tall."

They looked into each other's eyes again and laughed. Then a voice spoke over their shoulders — a kind, patient voice. "Oh, Laviny," it said; "I wouldn't bet if I was you."

Lavinia gave a little scream. Both turned instantly. The young man who had been watching them stood close to them. He wore working-clothes — a flannel shirt and cheap-faded trousers and coat. He had a good, strong, honest face, and there was a tenderness in the look he bent on the girl that struck Diller as being almost pathetic.

The glow in Lavinia's face turned to the scarlet of the sunset.

"*Oh!*" she said, embarrassedly. "That you, Bart? I didn't know you was back."

"I just got back," he replied, briefly. "I got to go back again in the mornin'. I was just on my way up to your house. I guess I'll go on. I'm tired, an' I've seen lots o' c'noe races." He looked at her wistfully.

"Well," she said, after a moment's hesitation. "You go on up, then. Maw an' paw's at home, an' I'll come as soon 's the race 's over."

"All right," he said, with a little drop in his voice, and walked away.

"Oh, *dear!*" cried Lavinia. "We're missin' the start, ain't we?"

The canoes were lying side by side, waiting for the signal. Every Indian was bent forward,

152

holding his paddle suspended above the water in both hands. There was what might be termed a rigid suppleness in the attitude. The dark outlines of the paddles showed clearly in the water, which had turned yellow as brass. Suddenly the band ceased playing and the signal rang across the sunset. Thirty-three paddles shot into the water, working with the swift regularity of piston-rods in powerful engines. The crowds cheered and yelled. The canoes did not flash or glide now, but literally plowed and plunged through the water, which boiled and seethed behind them in white, bubbled foam that at times completely hid the bronze figures from sight. There was no shouting now, but tense, breathless excitement. People clung motionless, in dangerous places and stared with straining eyes, under bent brows, after the leaping canoes. The betting had been high. The fierce, rhythmic strokes of the paddles made a noise that was like the rapid pumping of a great ram. To Diller, who stood, pale, with compressed lips, it sounded like the frantic heart-beat of a nation in passionate riot. Mingled with it was a noise that, once heard, cannot be forgotten — a weird, guttural chanting on one tone, that yet seemed to hold a windy, musical note ; a sound, regular, and rhythmic as the paddle-strokes, that came from deep in the breasts of the rigidly swaying Indians and found utterance through locked teeth.

A mile out a railroad crossed the tide-lands, and this was the turning point. The Nooksacks made it first, closely followed by the Alaskans, and then, amid wild cheering, the three canoes headed for the viaduct. Faster and faster worked those powerful arms; the paddles whizzed more fiercely through the air; the water spurted in white sheets behind; the canoes bounded, length on length, out of the water; and louder and faster the guttural chant beat time. The Alaskans and the Nooksacks were coming in together, carven prow to carven prow, and the excitement was terrific. Nearer and nearer, neither gaining, they came. Then, suddenly, there burst a mad yell of triumph, and the Alaskan boat arose from the water and leaped almost its full length ahead of the Nooksack's; and amidst waving hats and handkerchiefs, and almost frantic cheering — the race was won.

"By the eternal!" said Diller, beginning to breathe again and wiping the perspiration from his brow. "If that isn't worth crossing the plains to see, I don't know what is!" But his companion did not hear. She was alternately waving her kerchief to the victors and pounding her small fists on the railing in an ecstasy of triumph.

"Lavin-*ee!*"

"Well?"

"You come right down hyeer an' help me em'ty this renchin'-water. I'd like to know what's got into you! A-stayin' up-stairs half your time, an' just a-mopin' around when you are down. You ain't b'en worth your salt lately!"

The girl came into the kitchen slowly. "What you jawin' about now, maw?" she said, smiling.

"I'll show you what I'm a-jawin' about, as you call it. Take holt o' this tub an' help me em'ty this renchin'-water."

"Well, don't holler so; Mr. Diller 'll hear you."

"I don't care 'f he *does* hear me. I can give him his come-up'ans if he goes to foolin' around, listenin'. I don't care 'f he does write for a paper in New York! You've got to take holt o' the work more'n you've b'en lately. A-traipsin' around all over the country with him, a-showin' him things to write about an' make fun of! I sh'u'd think Bart Winn had just about got enough of it."

"I wish you'd keep still about Bart Winn," said Lavinia, impatiently.

"Well, I ain't a-goin' to keep still about him." Mrs. Vaiden poured the dish-water into the sink and passed the dish-cloth round and round the pan, inside and outside with mechanical care, be-

155

fore she opened the back door and hung it out on the side of the house. "I guess I don't haf to ask *you* when I want to talk. There you was — gone all day yeste'day a-huntin' star-fish, an' that renchin'-water a-settin' there a-ruinin' that tub because I couldn't em'ty it all myself. Just as if he never saw star-fish where he come from. An' then to-day — b'en gone all the mornin' a-ketchin' crabs ! How many crabs 'd you ketch, I'd like to know !"

"We didn't ketch many," said Lavinia, with a soft, aggravating laugh. "The water wa'n't clear enough to see 'em."

"No, I guess the water *wa'n't* clear enough to see 'em !" The rinsing-water had been emptied, and Mrs. Vaiden was industriously wiping the tub. "I've got all the star-fishin' an' the crab-ketchin' I want, an' I'm a-goin' to tell that young man that he can go some'ers else for his board. He's b'en here a month, an' he's just about made a fool o' you. Pret' soon you'll be a-thinkin' you're too good for Bart Winn."

"Oh, no," said Bart Winn's honest voice in the doorway ; "I guess Laviny won't never be a-thinkin' that."

"Mercy !" cried Mrs. Vaiden, starting and coloring guiltily. "That you ? How you scairt me ! I'm all of a-trimble."

Bart advanced to Lavinia and kissed her with

much tenderness ; but instead of blushing, she paled.

"When 'd you come?" she asked, briefly, drawing away, while her mother, muttering something about the sour cream and the spring-house, went out discreetly.

"This mornin'," said Bart. "I'm a-goin' to stay home now."

The girl sat down, taking a pan of potatoes on her lap. "I wonder where the case-knife is," she said, helplessly.

"I'll get it," said Bart, running into the pantry and returning with the knife. "I love to wait on you, Laviny," he added, with shining eyes. "I guess I'll get to wait on you a sight, now. I see your paw 's I come up an' he said as how I could board hyeer. I'll do the shores for you — an' glad to. An', oh, Laviny! I 'most forgot. I spoke for a buggy 's I come up, so's I can take you a-ridin' to-night."

"I guess I can't go," said Lavinia, holding her head down and paring potatoes as if her life depended upon getting the skins off.

"You can't? Why can't you?"

"I—why, I'm goin' a salmon-spearin' up at Squalicum Creek, I guess. Salmon's a-runnin' like everything now. 'Most half the town goes there soon 's it gets dark."

"That a fact?" said Bart, shifting from one

157

foot to the other and looking interested. "I want to know! Well" — his face brightened — "I'll go down an' tell 'em I'll take the rig to morro' night, an' I'll go a-spearin' with you. Right down in front o' Eldridge's?"

"Yes." A pulse began thumping violently in the girl's throat. Her eyelids got so heavy she could not lift them. "I guess — that is, I — why, you see, Bart, I got comp'ny."

"Well, I guess the girls won't object to my goin' along o' you."

"It ain't girls," said Lavinia, desperately. "It's — a — it's Mr. Diller; the gentleman that boards here."

"Oh," said Bart, slowly. Then there was a most trying silence, during which the ticking of the clock and the beating of her own heart were the only sounds Lavinia heard. At last she said, feebly: "You see he writes for a New York newspaper — one o' the big ones. He's a-writin' up the whole Puget Sound country. An' he don't know just what he'd ort to see, nor just how to see it, unless somebody shows him about — an' I've b'en a-showin' him."

"Oh!" said Bart again, but quite in another tone, quite cheerfully. "That's it, is 't, Laviny? Well, that's all right. But I'll be hanged if you didn't take my breath away for a minute. I thought you meant—Laviny!"—a sudden seriousness came into his tone and look—"I guess you don't know how much I think o' you. My heart's just *set* on you, my girl—my whole life's wrapped up in you." He paused, but Lavinia did not speak or look at him, and he added, very slowly and thoughtfully—"I reckon it 'u'd just about kill me, 'f anything happened to you."

"I guess nothin' 's a-goin' to happen." She dropped one potato into a pan of cold water and took up another.

"No, I guess not." He took on a lighter tone. "But I'll tell you what, Laviny! If that's all, he ain't comp'ny at all; so you can just tell him I'm a-goin', too." He came closer and laid a large but very gentle hand on her shoulder. "You might even tell him I've got a right to go, Laviny."

The girl shrank, and glanced nervously at the door.

"I wouldn't like to do that, Bart. After his arrangin' to go, an' a-hirin' the skiff hisself. *I* don't know but what he's got somebody else to go along of us."

"Why, does he ever?"

"Well, I don't recollect that he ever has; but then he might of, this time, I say, for all I know."

There was another silence. Then the big hand patted the girl's shoulder affectionately and the

159

honest eyes bent on her the look of patient tenderness that Diller had considered pathetic.

"All right, Laviny ; you go along of him, just
by yourself, an' I'll stop home with your paw an'
your maw. I want you to know, my girl, that I
trust you, an' believe every word you say to me.
I ain't even thought o' much else besides you
ever sence I saw you first time at the liberry sociable, an' I won't ever think o' much else, I
don't care what happens. Bein' afraid to trust a
body 's a poor way to show how much you think
about 'em, is my religion ; so you go an' have a
good time, an' don't you worry about me." He
tucked one of her runaway curls behind her ear
awkwardly. "I'll slip down to the liv'ry stable
now, an' tell 'em about the rig."

"All right," said Lavinia.

Her mother came in one door, after a precau-
tionary scraping of her feet and an alarming
paroxysm of coughing, and looked rather disappointed to see Bart going out at the other, and to
realize that her modest warnings had been thrown
away. "Well, 'f I *ever !* " she exclaimed. "Laviny Vaiden, whatever makes you *look* so? You
look just 's if you'd seen a spook! You're a
kind 'o yellow-gray—just like you had the
ja'ndice ! What *ails* you?"

"I got a headache," said the girl ; and then,
somehow, the pan slid down off her lap, and the

potatoes and the parings went rolling and sprawl-
ing all over the floor ; Lavinia's head went down
suddenly on the table, and she was sobbing bitterly.

Her mother looked at her keenly, without speaking, for a moment ; then she said dryly, " Why,
I guess you must have an awful headache. Come
on kind o' sudden like, didn't it ? I guess you'd
best go up and lay down, an' I'll bring a mustard
plaster up an' put on your head. Ain't nothin'
like a plaster for a headache — 'specially that kind
of a headache."

Bart Winn walked into the livery stable with an
air of indifference put on so stiffly that it deceived
no one. It was not that he did not feel perfectly
satisfied with Lavinia's explanation, but he was
a trifle uneasy lest others should not see the thing
with his eyes.

" I guess I won't want that rig to-night, Billy,"
he said, pulling a head of timothy out of a bale
of hay that stood near. " I'll take it to-morro'
night."

"All right," said the young fellow, with a smile
that Bart did not like. " Girl sick, aigh ?"

" No," said Bart, softly stripping the fuzz off
the timothy.

" Well, I guess I understan'," said Billy, winking one eye, cheerfully. " I've b'en there myself. Girls is as much alike 's peas — *sweet*-peas "

—he interjected with a hearty laugh —"in a pod, the world over. It ain't never safe for a fellow to come home, after bein' away a good spell, an' engage a buggy before findin' out if the girl ain't engaged to some other fello'— it ain't noways *safe*. I smiled in my sleeve when you walked in so big an' ordered your'n."

Bart Winn was slow to anger, but now a dull red came upon his face and neck, and settled there as if burnt into the flesh. His eyes looked dangerous, but he spoke quietly. "I guess you don't know what you're talkin' about, Billy. I guess you hadn't best go any furder."

Billy came slowly toward him, nettled by his tone — by its very calm, in fact. "D' you mean to say that Laviny Vaiden ain't goin' a-salmon-spearin' to-night with that dandy from New York?"

Bart swallowed once or twice.

"I don't mean to say anything that's none o' your business," he said.

"Well, she's been a-spearin' with him ev'ry night sence the salmon's b'en a-runnin', anyway."

The strong, powerful trembling of a man who is trying to control himself now siezed Bart Winn.

"If you're goin' to put on airs with me," continued Billy, obtusely, "I'll just tell you a few *fax !* They don't burn any torch in their boat, an'

162

they don't spear any salmon! That's just a blind.
They go off by theirselves — clear away from the
spearers, an' they don't come back till they see
the torches a-goin' out an' know that we all's
a-goin' home. It's the town talk. Not that they
say anything wrong, for we've all knowed Laviny
sence she was a baby ; but it's as plain as the nose
on a man's face that you ain't in it there since that
dood come.''

A panorama of colors flamed over Bart's face ;
his hands clenched till the nails cut into the flesh
and the blood spurted ; who has seen the look in
the eyes of the lion that cowers and obeys under
the terrible lash of the trainer will know the look
that was in the man's eyes while the lash of his
own will conquered him ; his broad chest swelled
and sunk. At last he spoke, in a deep, shaking
voice. "Billy," he said, "you're a liar — a liar !
Damn you !'' He struggled a moment longer
with himself, and then turned and hurried away
as if possessed of the devil.

But Billy followed him to the door and called
after him —"Oh, damn me, aigh? Now, I don't
want I sh'u'd have a fight with you, Bart. I was
tryin' to do you a favor. If you think I'm a
liar, it's a mighty easy thing for you to go down
there to-night an' see for yourself. That's all *I*
ask.''

Bart went on in a passion of contending emo-

163

tions. "He's a liar! He's a liar!" he kept saying, deep in his throat; but all the time he had the odd feeling that somebody, or something, was contradicting him. A warm wind had arisen, and it beat against his temples so persistently that they felt numb by the time he reached the Vaiden's. He cleaned his boots on the neat mat of gunny-sacking laid at the door for that purpose, and entered the kitchen. "Where's Laviny?" he asked.

"She's up-stairs with a headache," replied Mrs. Vaiden, promptly.

"It must 'a' come on sudden."

"Yes, I guess it must." Mrs. Vaiden spoke cautiously. She was sure there had been a quarrel, and she was afraid her own remark, overheard by Bart, had brought it on.

"Well, I want to see her."

"Right away?"

"Yes," said Bart, after a little hesitation, "right away, I reckon."

Mrs. Vaident went up-stairs, and returned presently, followed by Lavinia. The girl looked pale; a white kerchief bound about her brow increased her pallor; her eyes were red. She sat down weakly in a splint-bottom chair and crossed her hands in her lap.

At sight of the girl's suffering, Bart knew instantly that he had been doubting her without realizing it, because his faith in her came back with such a strong rush of tenderness.

"Sick, Laviny?" he asked, in a tone that was a caress of itself—it was so very gentle a thing to come from so powerful a man.

"I got a headache," said Lavinia, looking at the floor. "It came on right after you left. It aches awful."

Bart went to her and laid his hand on her shoulder. It was a strong hand to be shaking so.

"Laviny, I'm a brute to get you up out o' bed ; but I'm more of a brute to 'a' believed "— He stopped, and she lifted her eyes, fearfully, to his face. "I've been listenin' to things about you."

"What things?" She looked at the floor again.

"Well, I ain't goin' to so much as ask you 'f it's so ; but I'm goin' to tell you how *mean* I've b'en to listen to 't an' to keep a-wonderin' if it c'u'd be so,—an' then see if you can forgive me. I've b'en hearin' that you don't light no torch nor ketch no salmon when you go a-spearin', but that you an' him go off by yourselves an' stay — an' that he — he"— the words seemed to stick in his throat —"he's cut me out."

After a little Lavinia said —"Is that all?"

"All ! Yes. Ain't that enough?"

"Yes, it's enough—plenty for you to 'a' believed about me. I wouldn't 'a' believed that much about you." The humor of this remark seemed to appeal to her, for she smiled a little. Then she got up. "But it's all right, Bart. I ain't mad. If that's all, I guess I'll go back to bed. You tell maw I couldn't put them roastin'-ears on—my head feels so."

He caught her to his breast and kissed her several times, with something like a prayer in his eyes, and with a strong, but sternly controlled passion that left him trembling and staggering like a drunken man when she was gone.

After Lavinia and Diller were gone that night Bart sat out on the kitchen steps, smoking his pipe. He stooped forward, his elbows resting on his knees. His right hand held the pipe, and the left supported his right arm. His eyes looked straight before him into the purple twilight. The wind had gone down, but now and then a little gust of perfume came around the corner from the wild clover, still in delicate pink blossom on the north side of the house. The stars came out, one by one, in the deep blue spaces above, and shrill mournful outcries came from winged things in the green depths of the ferns. Already the torches of the salmon-spearers were beginning to flare out from the shadow of the cliffs across the bay. Mr.

Vaiden was not at home, but Mrs. Vaiden was walking about heavily in the kitchen, finishing the evening work.

Mrs. Vaiden was not quite easy in her mind. She really liked Bart Winn, but, to be unnecessarily and disagreeably truthful, she liked even better his noble donation claim, which he was now selling off in town lots. Time and time again during the past month she had cautioned Lavinia to not " go galivantin' 'round with that Diller so much ; " and on numerous occasions she had affirmed that " she'd *bet* Laviny would fool along till she let Bart Winn slip through her fingers, after all." Still, it had been an unconfessed satisfaction to her to observe Mr. Diller's frank admiration for her daughter—to feel that Lavinia could "have her pick o' the best any day." She knew how this rankled in some of the neighbors' breasts. She wished now that she had been more strict. She said to herself, as she went out to the spring-house: " I wish I'd 'a' set my foot right down on his goin' a step with her. An' there I started it myself, a-sendin' her off to that c'noe race with him, just to tantalize Mis' Bentley an' her troop o' girls. But land knows I never dreamt o' its goin' on this way. What's a newspaper fello' compared to a donation claim, *I'd* like to know ? "

At nine o'clock she went to the door and said, in that tone of conciliatory tenderness which

167

comes from a remorseful conscience: "Well, Bart, I guess I'll go to bed. I'm tired. You goin' to set up for Laviny?"

"Yes," said Bart; "good-night."

"Well, good-night, Bart." She stood holding a lighted candle in one hand, protecting its flame from the night air with the other. "I reckon they'll be home by ten."

"I reckon so."

At the top of the stairs Mrs. Vaiden remembered that the parlor windows were open, and she went back to close them. The wind was rising again, and as she opened the parlor door it puffed through the open windows and sent the curtains streaming out into the room; then it went whistling on through the house, banging the doors.

After a while quiet came upon the house. Bart sat smoking silently. The Vaidens lived on a hill above the town, and usually he liked to watch the chains of electric lights curving around the bay; but to-night he watched the torches only. Suddenly he flung his pipe down with a passionate movement and stood up, reaching inside the door for his hat. But he sat down again as suddenly, shaking himself like a dog, as if to fling off something that was upon him. "No; I'm damned if I will!" he said in his throat. "I *won't* watch her! She said it wa'n't so, an' I believe her." But he did not smoke again, and he breathed more heavily as the moments ticked by and she did not come. At half-past ten Mrs. Vaiden came down in a calico wrapper and a worsted shawl.

"Why, ain't she come *yet?*" she asked, holding the candle high and peering under it at the back of the silent figure outside.

"No," said Bart quietly; "she ain't."

"Why, it's half-after ten! She never's b'en out this a-way before. D'you think anything c'u'd 'a' hapened?"

"No," said Bart, slowly; "I guess they'll be along."

"Well, I don't want that she sh'u'd stay out till this time o' night with anybody but you. She's old enough to know better. It don't look well."

"It looks all right, as fur as that goes," said Bart.

"Oh, if *you* think so."

Mrs. Vaiden lowered the candle huffily.

Bart arose and came inside. He was pale but he spoke calmly, and he looked her straight in the eyes.

"It's all right as fur as she goes; I'd trust her anywheres. But how about him? What kind of a man is he?"

"Oh, I don't know," said Mrs. Vaiden, weakly.

169

"How d' you expect me to know what kind of a *man* he is? He's a nice-appearin', polite sort of a fello', an' he writes for a newspaper 'n New York — one o' them big ones. But he don't seem to me to have much backbone or stand-upness about him. I sh'u'd think he's one o' them that never *intends* to do anything wrong, but does it just because its pleasant for the time bein', and then feels sorry for 't afte'ards."

Bart's brows bent together blackly.

"But I must say"— Mrs. Vaiden's tone gathered firmness —"you might pattern after him a little in politeness, Bart. I think Laviny likes it. He's alwus openin' gates for her, an' runnin' to set chairs for her when she comes into a room, an' takin' off his hat to her, an' carryin' her umberella, an' fetchin' her flow'rs; an' I b'lieve he'd most die before he'd walk on the inside o' the sidewalk or go over a crossin' ahead o' her. An' I can see Laviny likes them things."

She put the candle on the table and huddled down into a chair.

The look of anger on the man's face gave place to one of keen dismay.

"I didn't know she liked such things. I never thought about 'em. I wa'n't brought up to such foolishness."

"Well, she likes 'em, anyhow. I guess most women do." Mrs. Vaiden sighed unconsciously.

"Why, Bart, it's a quarter of, an' she ain't here yet. D' you want I sh'u'd go after her?"

"No, I don't want you sh'u'd go after her. I want you sh'u'd let her alone, an' show her we got confidence in her. She's just the same as my wife, an' I don't want her own mother sh'u'd think she'd do anything she hadn't ort to."

Mrs. Vaiden's feelings were sensitive and easily hurt; and she sat now in icy silence, looking at the clock. But when it struck eleven she thawed, being now thoroughly frightened."

"Oh, Bart, I do think we'd best look in her room. She might 'a' got in someway without our hearin' her — an' us settin' hyeer like a couple o' bumps on a lawg."

"She might 'a'," said Bart, as if struck by the suggestion. "You get me a candle an' I'll go up and see. You stay here," he added, over his shoulder, as he took the candle and started.

"Look out!" she cried, sharply, as the blue flame plowed a gutter down one side of the candle. "Don't hold it so crooked! You'll spill the sperm onto the stair-carpet!"

It was with a feeling of awe that Bart went into the dainty little room. There were rosebuds on the creamy wall-paper, and the ceiling, slanting down on one side, was pale, pale blue, spangled with silver stars; the windows were closed, and thin, soft curtains fell in straight folds

171

over them; the rag carpet was woven in pink-
and-cream stripes; there was a dressing-table
prettily draped in pink. For a moment the man's
love was stronger than his anxiety; the prayer
came back to his eyes as he looked at the narrow,
snowy bed.

Then he went to the dressing-table and saw a
folded slip of paper with his name upon it.

After a while he became conscious that he had
read the letter a dozen times, and still had not
grasped its meaning. He stooped closer to the
candle and read it again, his lips moving mechanically:

"DEAR BART:—I'm goin' away. I'm goin' with
him. I told you what wa'n't so this mornin'. I do like
him the best. I couldn't have you after knowin' him.
I feel awful bad to treat you this a-way, but I haf to.
                                                LAVINY."
"P. S.—I want that you sh'u'd marry somebody else
as soon as you can, an' be happy."

A querulous call came from the hall below.
He took the candle in one hand and the letter in
the other and went down, stumbling clumsily on
the stairs. A great many noises seemed to be
ringing in his head, and the sober paper with
which the walls of the hall were covered to have

172

suddenly taken on great scarlet spots. He felt helpless and uncertain in his movements, as if he had no will to guide him. He must have carried the candle very crookedly, for Mrs. Vaiden, who was watching him from below, cried out, petulantly: "There, you *are* spillin' the sperm! Just look at you!" But she stopped abruptly when she saw his face.

"Why, whatever on this earth!" she exclaimed, solemnly. "What you got there? A letter?"

"Yes." He set the candle on the table and held the letter toward her. "It's from Laviny."

"From Laviny! Why, what on earth did she write to you about?"

He burst into wild, terrible laughter. "She wants I sh'u'd marry somebody else as soon as I can, an' be happy." These words, at least, seemed to have written themselves on his brain. He groped about blindly for his hat, and went out into the shrill, whistling night. The last torch had burnt itself out, and everything was black save the electric lights, winking in the wind, and one strip of whitening sky above Mount Baker, where presently the moon would rise, silver and cool.

It was seven o'clock in the morning when he came back. He washed his hands and face at the

sink on the porch, and combed his hair before a
tiny mirror, in which a dozen reflections of himself danced. Mrs. Vaiden was frying ham. At
sight of him she began to cry, weakly and noiselessly. "Where you been?" she sniffled. "You
look forty year old. I set up till one o'clock.
a-waitin' for you."

"Mrs. Vaiden," said Bart, quietly, "I'm in
great trouble. I've walked all night, tryin' to
make up my mind to 't. I've done it at last ;
but I cu'dn't 'a' come back tell I did. I'm sorry
you waited up."

"Oh, I don't mind that as long as you're gettin' reconciled to 't, Bart." Mrs. Vaiden spoke
more hopefully. "You set right down an' have
a bite to eat."

"I don't want anything," he replied ; but he
sat down and took a cup of coffee. It must have
been very hot, for suddenly great tears came into
his eyes and stood there. Mrs. Vaiden sat down
opposite to him and leaned her elbow on the table
and her head on her hand. "Bart," she said,
solemnly, "I don't want you sh'u'd think I ever
winked at this. It never entered my head. My
heart's just broke. To see a likely girl, that c'u'd
'a' had her pick anywheres, up an' run away with
a no-account newspaper fello' — when she c'u'd
'a' had you !" The man's face contracted.
"Whatever on earth the neighbors 'll say I don't
know."   174

"Who cares what neighbors say?"

"Oh, that's all very well for you to say; you ain't her mother."

"No," said Bart, with a look that made her quail; "I ain't. I wish to God I was! Mebbe 't wouldn't *hurt* so!"

"Well, it 'ad ort to hurt more!" retorted the lady, with spirit. "Just 's if you felt any worse 'n I do!" He laid his head on his hand and groaned. "Oh, I know it's gone deep, Bart" — her tone softened — "but 's I say, you ain't her mother. You'll get over it an' marry agair — like Laviny wanted that you sh'u'd. It was good o' her to think o' that. I will say that much for her."

"Yes," said Bart; "it was good of her." Then there came a little silence, broken finally by Mrs. Vaiden. Her voice held a note of peevish regret. "There's that fine house o' your'n 'most finished—two story an' a ell! An' that liberry across the front hall from the parlor! When I think how vain Laviny was o' that liberry! What'll you do with the house, now, Bart?"

"Sell it!" he answered, between his teeth.

"An' there's all that fine furnitur' that Laviny an' you picked out. She fairly danced when she told me about it. All covered with satin—robinegg green, wa'n't it?"

"Blue." The word dropped mechanically from his white lips.

"Well, blue, then. What'll you do with it?"

"I guess they'll take it back by my losin' my first payment," he answered, with a kind of ghastly humor.

"Well, there's your new buggy—all paid for. They won't take that back."

"I'll give that to you," he said, with a bitter smile.

"Oh, you!" exclaimed Mrs. Vaiden, throwing out her large hand at him in a gesture of mingled embarrassment and delight. "As if I'd take it, after Laviny's actin' up this a-way!"

He did not reply, and presently she broke out, angrily, with:

"The huzzy! The ungrateful, deceitful jade! To treat a body so. How do we know whether he's got anything to keep a wife on? I'll admit, though, he was alwus genteel-dressed. I do think, Bart, you might 'a' took pattern 'n that. 'T wa'n't like as if you wa'n't able to wear good clo'es—an' Laviny liked such things."

"I wish you'd 'a' told me a good spell ago what she liked, Mrs. Vaiden."

"Well, that's so. There ain't much use 'n lockin' the stable door after the horse 's gone. Oh, that makes me think about your offerin' me that buggy—'s if I w'u'd!"

176

"I guess you'll have to. I'm goin' to leave on the train, an' I'll order it sent to you."

"Oh, you! Why, where you goin', Bart?"

"I'm goin' to follow *him!*" he thundered, bringing his fist down on the table in a way that made every dish leap out of its place. "I ain't goin' to hurt him—unless talk hurts—but I'm goin' to say some *things* to him. I ain't had a thought for three year that that girl ain't b'en in! I ain't made a plan that she ain't b'en in. I've laid awake night after night just too happy to sleep. An' now to have a—a *thing* like him take her from me in one month. But that ain't the worst!" he burst out, passionately. "We don't know how he'll treat her, an' she'll be too proud to complain—"

"I can't see why you care how he treats her," said Mrs. Vaiden, "after the way she's treated you."

"No," he answered, with a look that ought to have crushed her, "I didn't s'pose you c'u'd see. I didn't expect you to see that, or anything else but your own feelin's — the way the thing affex you. But that's what I'm goin' to follow him for, Mrs. Vaiden. An' when I find him — I'm goin' to tell him"— there was an awful calm in his tone now — "that if he ever misuses her, now that he's married her, I'll kill him. I'll shoot him down like a dawg!"

"My Lord!" broke in Mrs. Vaiden, with a new thought. "What if he ain't married her! She never said so 'n her letter. Oh, Bart!" beginning to weep hysterically. "Mebbe you c'u'd get her back."

He leaped to his feet panting like an animal; his great breast swelled in and out swiftly, his hands clenched, his eyes burned at her.

"What!" he said. "Do you *dare? Her mother!* Oh, you — you — God! but I wish you was a man!"

The whistle of a coming train broke across the morning stillness. He turned, seized his hat and crushed it on his head. Then he came back and took up the chair in which he had been sitting.

"Mrs. Vaiden," he said, quietly, "d' you see this chair? Well, if he ain't married her —"

With two or three movements of his powerful wrists he wrenched the chair into as many pieces and dropped them on the floor.

After a while Mrs. Vaiden emerged from the stupefaction into which his last words had thrown her, and resumed her breakfast.

"Well," she said, stirring her coffee until it swam round and round in a smooth eddy in the cup, "if I ever see his beat! Whoever 'd 'a' thought he'd take his cuttin'-out that a-way? I never 'd

178

'a' thought it. Worryin' about her, after the way she's up and used him! A body 'd think he'd be glad if she was treated shameful, and hatto lead a mis'rable life a-realizin' what she'd threw away. But not him. Well, they say still water runs deep. Mebbe it's ungrateful to think it after his givin' me that fine buggy —(How Mis' Bentley will stare when I drive roun' to see her!" she interjected with a smile of anticipation.) "But after seein' how he showed up his temper just now I ain't sure but Laviny's head was level when she took the other 'n. 'F *only* he had a donation claim!"

ZARELDA

ZARELDA

"'Reldy! Say, 'Reldy! Za-*rel*-dy!"

The girl was walking rapidly, but she stopped at once and turned. She wore a cheap woolen dress of a dingy brown color. The sleeves were soiled at the wrists, but the narrow, inexpensive ruffle at the neck was white and fresh. Her thick brown hair was well brushed and clean. It was woven into a heavy, glistening braid which was looped up and tied with a rose-colored ribbon. Her shoes were worn out of shape and "run down" at the heels, and there were no gloves on the roughened hands clasped over the handle of her dinner-bucket.

"Oh, you?" she said, smiling.

"Yes, me," said the other girl, with a high color, as she joined Zarelda. They walked along briskly together. "I've been tryin' to ketch up with you for three blocks. Ain't you early?"

"No; late. Heard the whistle blow 'fore I left home. Didn't you hear it? Now own up, Em Brackett."

"No, I didn't—honest," said the other girl, laughing. "I set the clock back las' night an' forgot to turn it ahead ag'in this mornin'."

This young woman's dress and manner differed

from her companion's. Her dress was cheap, but of flimsy, figured goods that under close inspection revealed many and large grease spots; the sleeves were fashionably puffed; and there were ruffles and frills and plaitings all over it. At the throat was a bit of satin ruffling that had once been pale blue. Half her hair had been cut off, making what she called her "bangs," and this was tightly frizzed over her head as far back as her ears. Her back hair—coarse and broken from many crimpings—was braided and looped up like Zarelda's, and tied with a soiled blue ribbon. She wore much cheap jewelry, especially amethysts in gaudy settings. She carried herself with an air and was popularly supposed by the young people of factory society to be very much of a belle and a coquette.

Zarelda turned and looked at her with sudden interest.

"What in the name o' mercy did you turn the clock back for?"

Em tossed her head, laughing and blushing.

"Never you mind what for, 'Reldy Winser. It ain't any 'o your funeral, I guess, if I did turn it back. I had occasion to—that's all. You wasn't at the dance up at Canemah las' night, was you?" she added suddenly.

"No, I wasn't. I didn't have anybody to go with. You didn't go, either, did you?"

"Unh-hunh; I did."

Em nodded her head, looking up the river to the great Falls, with dreamy, remembering eyes. "We had a splendid time, an' the walk home along the river was just fine."

"Well, I could of gone with you if I'd of knew you was goin'. Couldn't I? Maw was reel well las' night, too."

She waited for a reply, but receiving none, repeated rather wistfully—"Couldn't I?"

Em took her eyes with some reluctance away from the river and looked straight before her.

"Why, I guess," she said, slowly and with slight condescension. "At least, I wouldn't of cared if my comp'ny wouldn't; an I guess"— with a beautiful burst of generosity—"he wouldn't of minded much."

"Oh," said Zarelda, "you had comp'ny, did you?"

"W'y, of course. You didn't s'pose I went up there all alone of myself, did you?"

"You an' me ust to go alone places, without any fellow, I mean," said Zarelda. A little color came slowly into her face. She felt vaguely hurt by the other's tone. "I thought mebbe you went with some o' the other girls."

"I don't go around that way any more." Em lifted her chin an inch higher. "When I can't have an—escort"—she uttered the word with some hesitation, fearing Zarelda might laugh at it—"I'll stay home."

Then she added abruptly in a reminiscent tone—"Maw acted up awful over my goin' with him. Thought for a spell I wouldn't get to go. But at last I flared all up an' told her if I couldn't go I'd just up an' leave for good. That brought her around to the whipple-trees double quick, I can tell you. I guess she won't say much agen my goin' with him another time."

"Goin' with who?" said Zarelda. Em looked at her, smiling.

"For the land o' love! D' you mean to say you don't know? I thought you'd of guessed. W'y, that's what made maw so mad—she was just hoppin', I tell you. That's what made her act up so. Said all the neighbors 'u'd say I was tryin' to get him away from you."

In an instant the blood had flamed all over Zarelda's face and neck.

"Get who away from me, Em Brackett?"

"As if there was so many to get!" said Em, laughing.

"Who are you a-talkin' about?" said Zarelda, sternly. Her face was paling now. "What of I got to do with you an' your comp'ny an' your maw's actin'-ups, I'd like to know. Who *was* your comp'ny?"

"Jim Sheppard; he"—

"Jim Sheppard!" cried Zarelda, furiously. She turned a white face to her companion, but her eyes were blazing. "What do I care for Jim Sheppard? Aigh? What do I care who he takes to dances up at Canemah? Aigh? You tell your maw, Em Brackett, that she needn't to trouble to act up on my account. She can save her actin'-ups for somebody that needs 'em! You tell her that, will you?"

"Well, I will," said Em, unmoved. "I'm glad you don't mind, 'Reldy. I felt some uneasy myself, seein' 's how stiddy he'd been goin' with you."

"Well, that don't hender his goin' with some-body else, does it? I ain't very likely to keep him from pleasin' hisself, am I?"

"Don't go to workin' yourself up so, 'Reldy. If you don't care, there's no use in flarin' up so. My! Just look at this em'rald ring in at Shindy's. Ain't that a beaut'?"

"I ain't got time." Zarelda walked on with her head up. "Don't you see we're late a'ready? The machin'ry's all a-goin', long ago."

The two girls pushed through the swinging gate and ran up the half-dozen steps to the entrance of the big, brick woolen mills. A young man in a flannel shirt and brown overalls was passing through the outer hall. He was twirling a full, crimson rose in his hand.

187

As the girls hurried in, he paused and stood awkwardly waiting for them, with a red face.

"Good mornin'," he said, looking first at Em and then, somewhat shamefacedly, at Zarelda.

"Good mornin', Jim," said Zarelda, coolly. She was still pale, but she smiled as she pressed on into the weaving-room. The many-tongued roar of the machinery burst through the open door to greet her. Em lingered behind a moment; and when she passed Zarelda's loom there was a crimson rose in her girdle and two more in her cheeks.

Five hours of monotonous work followed. Zarelda stood patiently by her loom, unmindful of the toilers around her and the deafening noise; she did not lift her eyes from her work. She was the youngest weaver in the factory and one of the most careful and conscientious.

The marking-room was in the basement, and in its quietest corner was a large stove whereon the factory-girls were permitted to warm their lunches. When the whistle sounded at noon they ceased work instantly, seized their lunch baskets, and sped — pushing, laughing, jostling — down the stairs to the basement. There was a small, rickety elevator at the rear of the factory, and some of the more reckless ones leaped upon it and let themselves down with the rope.

Zarelda was timid about the elevator; but that

noon she sprang upon it and giving the rope a
jerk went spinning down to the ground. As she
entered the marking-room one of the overseers
saw her. "What!" he exclaimed. "Did you
come down that elevator, 'Reldy? I thought you
had more sense 'n some o' the other girls. Why, it
ain't safe! You're liable to get killed on it."

"I don't care," said Zarelda, with a short, contemptuous laugh. "I'd just as soon go over the
falls in an Indian dug-out."

"You must want to shuffle off mighty bad,"
said the overseer. Then he added kindly, for he
and all the other overseers liked her — "What's
got into you, 'Reldy? Anything ail you?"

"No," said the girl; "nothin' ails me." But
his kind tone had brought sudden, stinging tears
to her eyes.

She went on silently to the stove and set her
bucket upon it. It contained thick vegetable
soup, which, with soda crackers, constituted her
dinner. She sat down to watch it, stirring it occasionally with a tin spoon. Twenty other girls
were crowding around the stove. Em was among
them. Zarelda saw the big red rose lolling in
her girdle. She turned her eyes resolutely away
from it, only to find them going back again and
again.

"Hey! Where 'd you get your rose at, Em
Brackett?" cried one of the girls.

"Jim Sheppard gave it to her," trebled another, before Em could reply. "I see him have it pinned onto his flannel shirt before the whistle blew."

"*Jim Sheppard!* Oh, my!"

There was a subdued titter behind Zarelda's back. She stirred the soup without lifting her eyes. "She went livid, though, an' then she went white!" one of the girls who read yellow novels declared afterward, tragically.

"Well," said Matt Wilson, sitting down on a bench and commencing to eat a great slice of bread thinly covered with butter, "who went to the dance up at Stringtown las' night?"

All the girls but two flung unclean hands above their heads. There was a merry outcry of "I did! I did!"

"Well, I didn't," said Matt. "My little lame sister coaxed me to wheel her down town, an' then it was too late."

"Why wasn't you there, Zarelda Winser?" cried Belle Church, opening her dinner bucket and examining the contents with the air of an epicurean.

For a second or two Zarelda wished honestly that she had a lame sister or an invalid mother. Then she said, quite calmly — "I didn't have any body to go with. That's why." She turned and faced them all as she spoke.

With a fine delicacy which was certainly not ac-

quired by education, every girl except Matt looked
away from Zarelda's face. Matt, not having been
to the dance, was not in the secret.

But Zarelda did not change countenance. She
sat calmly eating her soup from the bucket with
the tin spoon. She took it noisily from the point
of the spoon ; it was so thick that it was like eating a vegetable dinner.

"Didn't have anybody to go with?" repeated
Matt, laughing loudly. "I call that good. A
girl that's had steady comp'ny for a year ! Com-
p'ny that's tagged her closer 'n her shadder ! An'
I did hear"— she shattered the shell of a hard-
boiled egg by hammering it on the bench, and began picking off the pieces — "that your maw was
makin' you up a whole trunkful o' new underclo's — all trimmed up with tattin' an' crochet an'
serpentine braid — with insertin' two inches wide
on 'em, too. You didn't have anybody to go
with, aigh ? What's the matter with Jim Sheppard?"

Zarelda set her eyes on the red rose, as if that
gave her courage.

"He took Em Brackett."

"Not much !" said Matt, turning sharply.
"Honest? Well, then, he only took her because
you couldn't go an' ast him to take her instid."

"Why, the idee !" exclaimed Em, coloring
angrily and fluttering until the rose almost fell

191

out of her girdle. "Zarelda Winser, you tell her that ain't so!"

"No, it ain't so," said Zarelda, composedly, finishing her soup and beginning on a soda cracker. "He didn't ask me at all. He asked Em hisself."

"My!" said Net Carter, who had not been giving attention to the conversation. "What larrapin' good lunches you do have, Em Brackett. Chicken sandwich, an' spiced cur'nts, an' cake! My!"

Em Brackett looked out of the cobwebbed window at a small dwelling between the factory and the river. "I wonder why Mis' Allen don't hide up that ugly porch o' her'n with vines," she said, frostily. In factory society "larrapin" was not considered a polite word and a snub invariably awaited the unfortunate young woman who used it. The line must be drawn.

When the whistle blew the girls started leisurely for the stairs. There would be fifteen minutes during which they might stand around the halls and talk to the young men. Zarelda fell back, permitting all to precede her. Em looked back once or twice to see where she was.

"Well, if that 'Reldy Winser ain't grit!" whispered Nell Curry to Min Aster. "Just as good as acknowledgin' he's threw off on her, an' her a-holdin' up her head that way. There ain't another girl in the factory c'u'd do that — without flinchin', too."

When Zarelda reached the first hall she looked about her deliberately for Jim Sheppard. It had been his custom to meet her at the head of the stairs and going with her to one of the windows over-looking the Falls, to talk until the second whistle sent them to their looms. With a resolute air she joined Em Brackett, who was looking unusually pretty with a flush of excitement on her face and a defiant sparkle in her eyes.

In a moment Jim Sheppard came in. He hesi-tated when he saw the two girls together. A dull red went over his face. Then he crossed the hall and deliberately ignoring Zarelda, smiled into Em's boldly inviting eyes and said, distinctly — "Em, don't you want to take a little walk? There's just time."

"Why, yes," said Em, with a flash of poorly concealed triumph. "'Reldy, if you're a-goin' on upstairs, would you just as lieve pack my bucket up?"

"I'd just as lieve." Zarelda took the bucket, and the young couple walked away airily.

This was the way the factory young men had of disclosing their preferences. It was considered quite proper for a young man and a young woman to "go together" for months, or even years, and for one to "throw off" on the other, when attracted by a fresher face, with no explanation or apology.

"Well," whispered Belle Church, "I guess there ain't one of us but's been threw off on some time or other, so we know how it feels. But this is worse. He's been goin' with her more'n a year — an then to stop off so sudden !"

"It's better to stop off sudden than slow," said Matt Wilson, with an air of grim wisdom. "It hurts worse, but it don't hurt so long. Well, if I ever ! Just look at that !"

Out of sheer pity Frank Haddon had sidled out of a group of young men and made his way hesitatingly to Zarelda. "'Reldy," he said, "don't you want to—want to—take a walk, too ?"

The girl's eyes flamed at him. She knew that he was pitying her, and she was not of a nature to accept pity meekly. "No !" she flashed out, with scorn. "I don't want to—want to "—mimicking his tone—" take a walk, too. If I did, I guess I know the road."

She went upstairs, holding her head high.

When Zarelda went home that evening she found the family already at the supper table. The Winsers were not very particular about their home manners.

"We don't wait on each other here," Mrs. Winser explained, frequently, with pride, to her neighbors. "When a meal's done, on the table it goes in a jiffy, an' such of us as is here, eat. I just put the things back in the oven an' keep 'em hot for them that ain't on hand.''

Zarelda was compelled to pass through the kitchen to reach the stairs.

"Well, 'Reldy," said her mother, "you're here at last, be you? Hurry up an' wash yourself. Your supper's in the oven, but I guess the fire's about out. It does beat all how quick it goes out. Paw, I do wish you'd hump yourself an' git some dry wood. It 'u'd try the soul of a saint to cook with that green stuff. Sap fairly *oozes* out of it !''

"I don't want any supper, maw," said Zarelda.

"You don't want any supper ! What ails you ? Aigh ?''

"I don't feel hungry. I got a headache."

She passed the table without a glance and went upstairs. Her mother arose, pushing back her chair with decision and followed her. When she reached Zarelda's room, the girl was on her knees before her trunk. She had taken out a small writing-desk and was fitting a tiny key in the lock. Her hat was still on her head, but pushed back.

She started when the door opened, and looked over her shoulder, flushing with embarrassment and annoyance. Then, without haste or nervousness, she replaced the desk and closing the trunk, stood up calmly and faced her mother.

"Why don't you want any supper?" Mrs. Winser took in the trunk, the desk, and the blush at one glance. "Be you sick?"

"I got a headache." Zarelda took off her hat and commenced drawing the pins out of her hair. She untied the red ribbon and rolled it tightly around three fingers to smooth out the creases.

"Well, you wasn't puttin' your headache 'n your writin'-desk, was you?"

"No, I wasn't."

"Now, see here, 'Reldy,'" said Mrs. Winser, very kindly, coming closer and resting one large hand on the bureau ; "there's somethin' ails you besides a headache, an' you ain't a-goin' to pull any wool over my eyes. You've hed lots an' lots o' headaches an' et your supper just the same. What ails you?"

"Nothin' ails me, maw."

"There does, too, somethin' ail you. I guess I know. Now, what is it? You might just as well spit it right out an' be done with it."

Zarelda was silent. She began brushing her hair with a dingy brush from which tufts of bristles had been worn in several places. Her mother watched her patiently for a few moments, then she said —"Well, 'Reldy, be you goin' to tell me what ails you?"

Still there was no reply.

"You ain't turned off in the fact'ry, be you?"
Zarelda shook her head.

"Well, then," said Mrs. Winser slowly, as if
reluctantly admitting a thought that she had
been repelling, "it's somethin' about Jim Sheppard."

The girl paled and brushed her hair over her
face to screen it from her mother's searching gaze.

"Have you fell out with him?"

"No, I ain't fell out with him. Hadn't you
best eat your supper before it gets cold, maw?"

"No, I hadn't best. I ain't a-goin' to budge a
blessed step out o' this here room tell I know what
ails you. Not if I have to stay here tell daylight."
After a brief reflection she added—"Now, don't
you tell me he's been cuttin' up any! I always
said he was a fine young man, an' I say so still."

"He ain't been cuttin' up any," said Zarelda.
"At least, not as I know of."

She laid down the brush and pushing her hair
all back with both hands, fronted her mother suddenly, pale but resolute.

"If you want to know so bad," she said, "I'll
tell you. He's threw off on me."

Mrs. Winser sunk helplessly into a chair.
"Threw off on you!" she gasped.

"Yes, threw off on me." Zarelda kept her

dry, burning eyes on her mother's face. "D' you feel any better for makin' me tell it?"

Certainly her revenge for the persecution was all that heart could desire. Her mother sat limp and motionless, save for the slow, mechanical sliding back and forth of one thumb on the arm of her chair.

After a while Zarelda resumed the hair-brushing, calmly. Then her mother revived.

"Who — who in the name of all that's merciful has he took up with now?" she asked, weakly.

"Em Brackett."

"What!" Mrs. Winser almost screamed. "That onery hussy! 'Reldy Winser, be you a-tellin' me the truth?"

"Yes, maw. He took her to the dance up at Canemah las' night, an' she told me about it this mornin!"

"The deceitful jade. Smiled sweet as honey at me when she went by. You'd of thought sugar wouldn't melt in her mouth. I answered her 's short as lard pie-crust — I'm glad of it now. Has he took her any place else?"

"He took her walkin' at noontime. Stepped right up when she was standin' alongside o' me an' never looked at me, an' ast her — right out loud so's all of 'em could hear, too."

"Well, he'd ought to be ashamed of hisself! After bein' your stiddy comp'ny for more'n a year

— well onto two years — an' a-lettin' all of us think he was serious !"

" He never said he was, maw."

" He never said he was, aigh ? 'Reldy Winser, you ain't got enough spunk to keep a chicken alive, let alone a woman ! ' He never said he was,' aigh ? Well, ain't he been a-comin' here three nights a week nigh onto two year, an' a-takin' you every place, an' never a-lookin' at any other girl ? An' didn't he give you an amyfist ring las' Christmas, an' a reel garnet pin on your birthday ? An' didn't he come here one evenin', a-laffin' an' a-actin' up foolish in a great way an' holler out — ' Hello, maw Winser ?' Now, don't you go a-tellin' me he never meant anything serious."

" Well, he never said so," said the girl, stubbornly.

" I don't care if he *never* said so. He acted so. Why, for pity's sake ! You've got a grease-spot on your dress. I never see you with a grease-spot before — you're so tidy. How'd you get it on ?"

" Oh, I don't know."

"Benzine 'll take it out. Well — I'm a-goin' to give him a piece o' my mind !"

Zarelda lifted her body suddenly. She looked tall. Her eyes flamed out their proud fire.

" Now, see here, maw," she said, "you don't

say a word to him — not a word. This ain't
your affair; it's mine. It's the fashion in fact'ry
society for a girl an' a fellow to go together, an'
give each other things, without bein' real engaged; an' she has to take her chances o' some
other girl gettin' him away from her. If he
wants to throw off on her, all he's got to do 's to
take some other girl to a dance or out walkin'.
An' then, if he's give her a ring or anything, it's
etiquette for her to send it back to him, an' he'll
most likely give it to the other girl. I don't think
it's right, an' I don't say but what it's hard — "
her voice trembled and broke, but she conquered
her emotion stubbornly and went on — "but it's
the way in fact'ry society. There ain't a girl in
the fact'ry but what's had to stand it some time
or other, an' I guess I can. You don't want me
to be a laffin'-stawk, do you ?"

"No, I don't." Her mother looked at her in
a kind of admiring despair. "But I never hear
tell of such fashions an' such doin's in all my
born days. It's shameful. Your paw an' me
'd set our minds on your a-marryin' him an' gettin' a home o' your own. It's been a burden off
o' our minds for a year past — "

"Oh, maw !"

"Just to feel that you'd be fixed so's you could
take care o' your little sisters in case we dropped
off. An' there I've went an' made up all them

underclo's!" She leaned her head upon her hand and sat looking at the floor with a forlornly reminiscent expression. "An' put tattin' on three sets, an' crochet lace on three, an' serpentine edgin' on three. An' inserting on all of 'em! That ain't the worst of it. Iv'e *worked his initial in button-hole stitch* on every blessed thing!"

"Oh, maw, you never did that, did you?"

"Yes, I did. An' what's more, I showed 'em all to old Miss Bradley, too."

"You might just as well of showed 'em to the whole town!" said poor Zarelda, bitterly.

"They looked so nice I had to show 'em to somebody."

"Sister," piped a little voice at the foot of the stairs, "Mis' Riley's boy 's come to find out how soon you're a-comin' over to set up with the sick baby."

"Oh, I'd clear forgot." Zarelda braided her hair rapidly. "Tell him I'll be over 'n a few minutes."

"Now, see here, 'Reldy," said her mother, getting up and laying her hand affectionately on the girl's arm, "you ain't a-goin' to budge a single step over there to-night. You just get to bed an' put an arnicky plaster on your forehead—"

Zarelda laughed in a kind of miserable mirth.

" Oh, you can laff, but it'll help lots. I'll go over an' set up with that baby myself."

"No, you won't, maw." She slipped the last pin in her hair and set her hat firmly on the glistening braids. "I said I'd set up with the baby, an' I will. I ain't goin' to shirk just because I'm in trouble."

She went out into the cool autumn twilight. Her mother followed her and stood looking after her with sympathetic eyes. At last she turned and went slowly into the poor and gloomy house; as she closed the door she put all her bitterness and disappointment into one heavy sigh.

The roar of the Falls came loudly to Zarelda as she walked along rapidly. The dog-fennel was still in blossom, and its greenish snow was drifted high on both sides of her path. Still higher were billows of everlasting flowers, undulating in the soft wind. The fallen leaves rustled mournfully as she walked through them. Some cows were feeding on the commons near by; she heard their deep breathing on the grass before they tore and crushed it with their strong teeth; she smelled their warm, fragrant breaths.

She came to a narrow bridge under the cottonwoods where she saw the Willamette, silver and beautiful, moving slowly and noiselessly between its emerald walls. The slender, yellow sickle of the new moon quivered upon its bosom.

Zarelda stood still. The noble beauty of the night — all its tenderness, all its beating passion — shook her to the soul. Her life stretched out before her, hard and narrow as the little path running through the dog-fennel — a life of toil and duty, of clamor and unrest, of hurried breakfasts, cold lunches and half-warm suppers, of longing for knowledge that would never be hers — the hard and bitter treadmill of the factory life.

A sob came up into her dry throat, but it did not reach her lips.

"I won't!" she said, setting her teeth together hard. "I hate people who whine after what they can't have, instead o' makin' the best o' what they've got."

She lifted her head and went on. Her face was beautiful; something sweeter than moonlight shone upon it. She walked proudly and the dry leaves whirled behind her.

IN THE BITTER ROOT MOUNTAINS

IN THE BITTER ROOT MOUNTAINS

"Go slow, boys, for God's sake! If we miss this landing, we are lost. The rapids begin just around that bend."

Four men stood upon a rude raft, and with roughly-made oars and long fir poles were trying to guide it out of the current of the swollen Clearwater River into a small sheltered inlet.

Both shores of the river rose abruptly to steep and terrible mountains. Not far above was the snow-line.

The men's faces were white and haggard, their eyes anxious, half desperate. Huddled upon a stretcher at one end of the raft was a young man, little more than a boy, whose pallid, emaciated face was turned slightly to one side. His eyes were closed; the long black lashes lay like heavy shadows upon his cheeks. The weak November sunshine, struggling over the fierce mountains, shone through his thin nostrils, turning them pink, and giving an unearthly look to the face. A collie crouched close beside him, shivering with fear, yet ever and anon licking the cold hand lying outside the gray blanket; occasionally he lifted his head and uttered a long, mournful howl. Each time the four men shuddered and exchanged looks of despair,— so humanly appealing was it, and so deeply did it voice the terrible dread in their own hearts.

It was now two months since they had left Seattle on a hunting expedition in the Bitter Root Mountains in Idaho. For six weeks they had been lost in those awful snow fastnesses. Their hunting dogs had been killed by wild beasts. Their twelve pack-ponies had been left to starve to death when, finding further progress on land impossible on account of the snow, they constructed a raft and started on their perilous journey down the Clearwater.

The cook had been sick almost the entire time, and their progress had been necessarily slow and discouraging. They had now reached a point where the river was so full of boulders and so swift that they could proceed no farther on the raft.

For several days the cook had been unconscious, lying in a speechless stupor; but when they had, with much danger and excitement, landed and made him comfortable in a protected nook, he suddenly spoke,— faintly but distinctly.

"Polly," he said, with deep tenderness, "lay your hand on my head. I guess it won't ache so, then."

The four men, looking at him, grew whiter. They could not look at each other. The dog, having already taken his place beside him, lifted his head and looked at him with pitiable eagerness.

" Oh, Polly !"— there was a heart-break in the voice,—" you don't know what I've suffered ! The cold, and then the fever ! The pain has been awful. Oh, I've wanted you so, Polly — I've wanted you so ! . . . But it's all right, now that I'm home again. . . . Where's the baby, Polly ? Oh, the nights that I've laid, freezing and suffering in the snow, just kept alive by the thought o' you an' the little man ! I knew it 'u'd kill you 'f I died—so I *w'u'dn't* give up ! An' now I'm here 't home again. Polly —— "

" We must fix some supper, boys," said Darnell, roughly, turning away to hide his emotion. " Let's get the fire started."

" We've just got enough for one more good meal," said Roberts, in a tremulous voice. " There's no game around here, either. Guide, you must try to find a way out of this before dark, so we can start early in the morning."

Without speaking, the guide obeyed. It was dark when he returned. The men were sitting by the camp-fire, eating their supper. The dog still lay by his master, from whom even hunger could not tempt him.

The three men looked at the guide. He sat

209

down and took his cup of coffee in silence. "Well," said Darnell, at last, "can we go on?"

"Yes," said the guide, slowly; "we can. In some places there'll be only a few inches' foothold; an' we'll hev to hang on to bushes up above us, with the river in some places hundreds o' feet below; but we can do it, 'f we don't get rattled an' lose our heads."

There was a deep and significant silence. Then Brotherton said, with white lips, "Do you mean that we can't take *him*?"

"That's what I mean." The guide spoke deliberately. He could not lift his eyes. Some of the coffee spilled as he lifted the cup to his lips. "We can't take a thing, 'cept our hands and feet,— not even a blanket. It'll be life an' death to do it, then."

There was another silence. At last Darnell said: "Then it is for us to decide whether we shall leave him to die alone while we save ourselves, or stay and die with him?"

"Yes," said the guide.

"There is positively not the faintest chance of getting him out with us?"

"By God, no!" burst forth the guide, passionately. "It seems like puttin' the responsibility on me, but you want the truth, an' that's it. He can't be got out. It's leave him an' save ourselves, or stay with him an' starve."

After a long while Roberts said, in a low voice : "He's unconscious. He wouldn't know we had gone."

"He cannot possibly live three days, under any circumstances," said Brotherton. "Mortification has already begun in his legs."

"Good God!" exclaimed Darnell, jumping up and beginning to walk rapidly forth and back, before the fire. "I must go home, boys! My wife — when I think of her, I am afraid of losing my reason! When I think what she is suffering——"

Brotherton looked at him. Then he sunk his face into both his hands. He, too, had a wife. The guide put down his coffee ; large tears came into his honest eyes. He had no wife, but there was one——

Roberts got up suddenly. He had the look of a tortured animal in his eyes. "Boys," he said, "my wife is dead. My life doesn't matter so much, but — I've three little girls! I *must* get back, somehow!"

The sick man spoke. They all started guiltily, and looked toward him. "Yes, yes, Polly," he said, soothingly, "I know how you worried about me. I know how you set strainin' your eyes out the window day an' night, watchin' fer me. But now I'm home again, an' it's all right. I guess you prayed, Polly ; an' I guess God heard you.

. . There's a boy fer you ! He knows me,
)o.''

The silence that fell upon them was long and
terrible. The guide arose at last, and, without
speaking, made some broth from the last of the
canned beef, and forced it between the sick man's
lips. When he came back to the fire, Darnell
took a silver dollar out of his pocket.

"Boys," he said, brokenly, "I don't want to
be the one to settle this, and I guess none of you
do. It is an awful thing to decide. I shall throw
this dollar high into the air. If it falls heads up,
we go ; tails — we stay."

The men had lifted their heads and were watching him. They were all very white ; they were all
trembling.

"Are you willing to decide it in this way?"

Each answered, "Yes."

"I swear," said Darnell, slowly and solemnly,
"that I will abide by this decision. Do you all
swear the same?"

Each, in turn, took the oath. Trembling now
perceptibly, Darnell lifted his hand slowly and
cast the piece of silver into the air. Their eyes
followed its shining course. For a second it disappeared ; then it came singing to the earth.

Like drunken men they staggered to the spot
where it had fallen, and fell upon their knees,
staring with straining eyes and bloodless lips.

"It is heads," said Darnell. He wiped the cold perspiration from his brow.

At that moment the dog lifted his head and sent a long, mournful howl to die in faint echoes in the mountains across the river.

At daylight they were ready to start. Snow lay on the ground to a depth of six inches. But a terrible surprise awaited them. At the last moment they discovered that the cook was conscious.

"You're not going — to leave me?" he said, in a whisper. His eyes seemed to be leaping out of their hollow sockets with terror.

"Only for a few hours," said Brotherton, huskily. "Only to find a way out of this, — to make a path over which we can carry you."

"Oh," he said, faintly; "I thought —— but you wouldn't. In the name o' God, don't leave me to die alone!"

They assured him that they would soon return. Then, making him as comfortable as possible, they went, — without hesitation, without one backward look. There was no noise. The snow fell softly and silently through the firs; the river flowed swiftly through its wild banks. The sick man lay with closed eyes, trustfully. But the dog knew. For the first time he left his master. He ran after them, and threw himself before them, moaning. His lifted eyes had a soul in them.

He leaped before them, and upon them, licking their hands and clothing ; he cast himself prone upon their feet, like one praying. No human being ever entreated for his life so passionately, so pathetically, as that dog pleaded for his master's.

At last, half desperate as they were, they kicked him savagely and flung him off. With a look in his eyes that haunted them as long as they lived, he retreated then to his master's side, and lay down in a heavy huddle of despair, still watching them. As they disappeared, he lifted his head, and for the last time they heard that long, heart-breaking howl.

It was answered by a coyote in the canyon above.

A week later the Associated Press sent out the following dispatch :

"The Darnell party, who were supposed to have perished in the Bitter Root Mountains, returned last night. Their hardships and sufferings were terrible. There is great rejoicing over their safe return. They were compelled to leave the cook, who had been sick the entire time, to die in the mountains. But for their determined efforts to bring him out alive, they would certainly have returned a month earlier."

The world read the dispatch and rejoiced with those rejoicing. But one woman, reading it, fell, as one dead, beside her laughing boy.

PATIENCE APPLEBY'S CONFESSING-UP

PATIENCE APPLEBY'S CONFESSING-UP

"It must be goin' to rain! My arm aches me so I can hardly hold my knitting needles."

"Hunh!" said Mrs. Wincoop. She twisted her thread around her fingers two or three times to make a knot; then she held her needle up to the light and threaded it, closing one eye entirely and the other partially, and pursing her mouth until her chin was flattened and full of tiny wrinkles. She lowered her head and looking at Mrs. Willis over her spectacles with a kind of good-natured scorn, said — "Is that a sign o' rain?"

"It never fails." Mrs. Willis rocked back and forth comfortably. "Like as not it begins to ache me a whole week before it rains."

"I never hear tell o' such a thing in all my days," said Mrs. Wincoop, with unmistakable signs of firmness, as she bent over the canton flannel night-shirt she was making for Mr. Wincoop.

"Well, mebbe you never. Mebbe you never had the rheumatiz. I've had it twenty year. I can't get red of it, anyways. I've tried the

Century liniment — the one that has the man riding over snakes an' things — and the arnicky, and ev'ry kind the drug-store keeps. I've wore salt in my shoes tell they turned white all over; and I kep' a buckeye in my pocket tell it wore a hole and fell out. But I never get red o' the rheumatiz."

Mrs. Wincoop took two or three stitches in silence; then she said — "Patience, now, she *can* talk o' having rheumatiz. She's most bent in two with it when she has it — and that's near all the time."

The rocking ceased abruptly. Mrs. Willis's brows met, giving a look of sternness to her face.

"That's a good piece o' cotton flannel," she said. "Hefty! Fer pity's sake! D' you put ruffles on the bottom o' Mr. Wincoop's night-shirt? Whatever d' you do that fer?"

"Because he likes 'em that way," responded Mrs. Wincoop, tartly. "There's no call fer remarks as I see, Mis' Willis. You put a pocket 'n Mr. Willis's, and paw never'd have that — never!" firmly.

"Well, I never see ruffles on a man's night-shirt before," said Mrs. Willis, laughing rather aggravatingly. "But they do look reel pretty, anyways."

"The longer you live the more you learn." Mis. Wincoop spoke condescendingly. "But

218

talking about Patience — have you see her lately?"

"No, I ain't." Mrs. Willis got up suddenly and commenced rummaging about on the table; there were two red spots on her thin face. "I'd most fergot to show you my new winter under-clo's. Ain't them nice and warm, though? They feel so good to my rheumatiz. I keep think-ing about them that can't get any. My, such hard times! All the banks broke, and no more prospect of good times than of a hen's being hatched with teeth! It puts me all of a trimble to think o' the winter here and ev'rybody so hard up. It's a pretty pass we've come to."

"I should say so. I don't see what Patience is a-going to live on this winter. She ain't fit to do anything; her rheumatiz is awful. She ain't got any fine wool underclo's."

Mrs. Willis sat down again, but she did not rock; she sat upright, holding her back stiff and her thin shoulders high and level.

"I guess this tight spell 'll learn folks to lay by money when they got it," she said, sternly. "I notice we ain't got any mortgage on our place, and I notice we got five thousand dollars in-vested. We got some cattle besides. We ain't frittered ev'rything we made away on foolishness, like some that I know of. We have things good and comf'terble, but we don't put on any style. Look at that Mis' Abernathy! I caught her teeheeing behind my back when I was buying red checked table clo's. Her husband a book-keeper! And her a-putting on airs over me that could buy her up any day in the week! Now, he's lost his place, and I reckon she'll come down a peg or two."

"She's been reel good to Patience, anyways," said Mrs. Wincoop.

Mrs. Willis knitted so fast her needles fairly rasped together.

"She takes her in jell and perserves right frequent. You mind Patience always liked sweet things even when her 'n' Lizy was girls together, Eunice."

It was so unusual for one of these two women to speak the other's name that they now exchanged quick looks of surprise. Indeed, Mrs. Wincoop seemed the more surprised of the two. But the hard, matter-of-fact expression returned at once to each face. If possible, Mrs. Willis looked more grim and sour than before the unwonted address had startled her out of her composure.

"Well," she said, scarcely unclosing her thin lips, "I reckon she had all the sweet things she was a-hankering after when she was a girl. I reckon she had a plenty and to spare, and I expect they got to tasting pretty bitter a good spell ago. Too much sweet always leaves a bit'rish taste in the mouth. My religion is — do what's right, and don't wink at them that does wrong. I've stuck to my religion. I reckon you can't get anybody to stand up and put their finger on anything wrong I've done — nor any of my fambly, either." Mrs. Wincoop put her hand on her chest and coughed mournfully. "Let them that's *sinned*," went on Mrs. Willis, lifting her pale, cold eyes and setting them full on her visitor, "make allowance fer sinners, say I. Mis' Abernathy, or Mis' Anybody Else, can pack all the clo's and all the sweet things they've got a mind to over to Patience Appleby; mebbe they've sinned, too — *I* don't know! But I do know that I ain't, and so I don't pack things over to her, even if she is all doubled up with the rheumatiz," unconsciously imitating Mrs. Wincoop's tone. "And I don't make no allowance for her sins, either, Mis' Wincoop."

A faint color came slowly, as if after careful consideration, to Mrs. Wincoop's face.

"There wa'n't no call fer you a-telling that," she said, with a great calmness. "The whole town knows you wouldn't fergive a sin, if your fergiving it 'u'd save the sinner hisself from being lost! The whole town knows what your religion is, Mis' Willis. You set yourself up and call yourself perfeck, and wrap yourself up in yourself —"

"There come the men — sh !" said Mrs. Willis. Her face relaxed, but with evident reluctance. She began to knit industriously. But the temptation to have the last word was strong.

"It ain't my religion, either," she said, her voice losing none of its determination because it was lowered. "I'd of fergive her if she'd a-confessed up. We all tried to get her to. I tried more 'n anybody. I told her"— in a tone of conviction —"that nobody but a brazen thing 'u'd do what she'd done and not confess up to 't — and it never fazed her. She *wouldn't* confess up."

The men were scraping their feet noisily now on the porch, and Mrs. Willis leaned back with a satisfied expression, expecting no reply. But Mrs. Wincoop surprised her. She was sewing the last pearl button on Mr. Wincoop's night-shirt, and as she drew the thread through and fastened it with scrupulous care, she said, without looking up — "I don't take much stock in confessings myself, Mis' Willis. I don't see just how confessings is good for the soul when they hurt so many innocent ones as well as the guilty ones. Ev'ry confessing affex somebody else ; and so I say if you repent and want to atone you can do 't without confessing and bringing disgrace on others. It's nothing but curiosity that makes people holler out — 'Confess-up now ! Confess-up now.' It ain't anybody's business but God's — and I reckon *He* knows when a body's sorry he's sinned and wants to do better, and I reckon He helps him just as much as if he got up on a church tower and kep' a-hollering out — 'Oh, good grieve, I've sinned! I've sinned!' — so 's the whole town could run and gap' at him! Mis' Willis, if some confessing-ups was done in this town that I know of, some people 'u'd be affected that 'u'd surprise you." Then she lifted up her voice cheerfully — "That you, father? Well, d' you bring the lantern? I reckon we'd best go right home; it's getting latish, and Mis' Willis thinks, from the way her arm aches her, that it's going to rain."

Mrs. Willis sat knitting long after Mr. Willis had gone to bed. Her face was more stern even than usual. She sat uncomfortably erect and did not rock. When the clock told ten, she arose stiffly and rolled the half finished stocking around the ball of yarn, fastening it there with the needles. Then she laid it on the table and stood looking at it intently, without seeing it. "I wonder," she said, at last, drawing a deep breath, "what she was a-driving at! I'd give a pretty to know."

"Mother, where's my Sund'y pulse-warmers at?"

223

"*I* don't know where your Sund'y pulse-warmers are at. Father, you'd aggravate a body into her grave! You don't half look up anything — and then begin asking me where it's at. What's under that bunch o' collars in your drawer? Looks some like your Sund'y pulse-warmers, don't it? This ain't Sund'y, anyways. Wa'n't your ev'ryday ones good enough to wear just to a church meeting?"

Mr. Willis had never been known to utter an oath; but sometimes he looked as if his heart were full of them.

"I reckon you don't even know where your han'ke'cher's at, father."

"Yes, I do, mother. I guess you might stop talking, an' come on now — I'm all ready."

He preceded his wife, leaving the front door open for her to close and lock. He walked stiffly, holding his head straight, lest his collar should cramp his neck or prick his chin. He had a conscious, dressed-up air. He carried in one hand a lantern, in the other an umbrella. It was seven o'clock of a Thursday evening and the bell was ringing for prayer-meeting. There was to be a church meeting afterward, at which the name of Patience Appleby was to be brought up for membership. Mrs. Willis breathed hard and deep as she thought of it.

She walked behind her husband to receive the

full light of the lantern, holding her skirts up
high above her gaiter-tops which were so large
and so worn as to elastic, that they fairly ruffled
around her spare, flat ankles. Her shadow danced
in piece-meal on the picket fence. After a while
she said —

"Father, I wish you wouldn't keep swinging
that lantern so ! A body can't see where to put
their feet down. Who's that ahead o' us ?"

"I can't make out yet."

"No wonder — you keep swinging that lantern
so ! Father, what does *possess* you to be so aggravating ? If I'd of asked you to swing it, you
couldn't of b'en *drug* to do it !"

Mrs. Willis was guiltless of personal vanity,
but she did realize the importance of her position
in village society, and something of this importance was imparted to her carriage as she followed
Mr. Willis up the church aisle. She felt that
every eye was regarding her with respect, and
held her shoulders so high that her comfortable
shawl fell therefrom in fuller folds than usual.
She sat squarely in the pew, looking steadily and
unwinkingly at the wonderful red velvet cross
that hung over the spindle-legged pulpit, her
hands folded firmly in her lap. She had never
been able to understand how Sister Wirth who
sat in the pew in front of the Willises, could always have her head a-lolling over to one side like

a giddy, sixteen-year-old. Mrs. Willis abominated such actions in a respectable, married woman of family.

Mr. Willis crouched down uneasily in the corner of the seat and sat motionless, with a self-conscious blush across his weak eyes. His umbrella, banded so loosely that it bulged like a soiled-clothes bag, stood up against the back of the next pew.

At the close of prayer-meeting no one stirred from his seat. An ominous silence fell upon the two dozen people assembled there. The clock ticked loudly, and old lady Scranton, who suffered of asthma, wheezed with every breath and whispered to her neighbor that she was getting so phthisicy she wished to mercy they'd hurry up or she'd have to go home without voting. At last one of the deacons arose and said with great solemnity that he understood sister Wincoop had a name to propose for membership.

When Mrs. Wincoop stood up she looked pale but determined. Mrs. Willis would not turn to look at her, but she caught every word spoken.

"Yes," said Mrs. Wincoop, "I want to bring up the name of Patience Appleby. I reckon you all know Patience Appleby. She was born here, and she's always lived here. There's them that says she done wrong onct, but I guess she's about atoned up for that — if any mortal living

226

has. I've know her fifteen year, and I don't know any better behaving woman anywheres. She never talks about anybody "— her eyes went to Mrs. Willis's rigid back —" and she never complains. She's alone and poor, and all crippled up with the rheumatiz. She wants to join church and live a Christian life, and I, fer one, am in favor o' us a-holding out our hand to her and helping her up."

"Amen!" shrilled out the minister on one of his upper notes. There was a general rustle of commendation — whispers back and forth, noddings of heads, and many encouraging glances directed toward sister Wincoop.

But of a sudden silence fell upon the small assembly. Mrs. Willis had arisen. Her expression was grim and uncompromising. At that moment sister Shidler's baby choked in its sleep, and cried so loudly and so gaspingly that every one turned to look at it.

In the momentary confusion Mr. Willis caught hold of his wife's dress and tried to pull her down ; but the unfortunate man only succeeded in ripping a handful of gathers from the band. Mrs. Willis looked down at him from her thin height.

"You let my gethers be," she said, fiercely. "You might of knew you'd tear 'em, a-taking holt of 'em that way !"

Then quiet was restored and the wandering eyes

227

came back to Mrs. Willis. "Brothers and sisters," she said, "it ain't becoming in me to remind you all what Mr. Willis and me have done fer this church. It ain't becoming in me to remind you about the organ, and the new bell, and the carpet fer the aisles — let alone our paying twenty dollars more a year than any other member. I say it ain't becoming in me, and I never 'd mention it if it wa'n't that I don't feel like having Patience Appleby in this church. If she does come in, *I* go out."

A tremor passed through the meeting. The minister turned pale and stroked his meagre whiskers nervously. He was a worthy man, and he believed in saving souls. He had prayed and plead with Patience to persuade her to unite with the church, but he had not felt the faintest presentiment that he was quarreling with his own bread and butter in so doing. One soul scarcely balances a consideration of that kind — especially when a minister has six children and a wife with a chronic disinclination to do anything but look pretty and read papers at clubs and things. It was small wonder that he turned pale.

"I want that you all should know just how I feel about it," continued Mrs. Willis. "I believe in doing what's right yourself and not excusing them that does wrong. I don't believe in having people like Patience Appleby in this church ; and she don't come in while *I'm* in, neither. That's all I got to say. I want that you all should understand plain that her coming in means my going out."

Mrs. Willis sat down, well satisfied. She saw that she had produced a profound sensation. Every eye turned to the minister with a look that said, plainly — "What have you to say to *that?*"

But the miserable man had not a word to say to it. He sat helplessly stroking his whiskers, trying to avoid the eyes of both Mrs. Wincoop and Mrs. Willis. At last Deacon Berry said — " Why, sister Willis, I think if a body repents and wants to do better, the church 'ad ort to help 'em. That's what churches are for."

Mrs. Willis cleared her throat.

" I don't consider that a body's repented, Deacon Berry, tell he confesses-up. Patience Appleby's never done that to this day. When she does, I'm willing to take her into this church."

" Brothers and sisters," said Mrs. Wincoop, in a voice that held a kind of cautious triumph, " I fergot to state that Patience Appleby reckoned mebbe somebody 'u'd think she'd ort to confess before she come into the church ; and she wanted I should ask the meeting to a'point Mis' Willis a committee o' one fer her to confess up to. Patience reckoned if she could satisfy Mis' Willis, ev'rybody else 'u'd be satisfied."

229

"Why — yes," cried the minister, with cheerful eagerness. "That's all right — bless the Lord!" he added, in that jaunty tone with which so many ministers daily insult our God. "I know Mrs. Willis and Patience will be able to smooth over all difficulties. I think we may now adjourn."

"Whatever did she do that fer?" said Mrs. Willis, following the lantern homeward. "She's got something in her mind, *I* know, or she'd never want me a'p'inted. Father, what made you pull my gethers out? D'you think you could make me set down when I'd once made up my mind to stand up? You'd ought to know me better by this time. This is my secon'-best dress, and I've only wore it two winters — and now look at all these gethers tore right out!"

"You hadn't ought to get up and make a fool o' yourself, mother. You'd best leave Patience Appleby be."

"You'd ort to talk about anybody a-making a fool o' hisself! After you a-pulling my gethers clean out o' the band — right in meeting! You'd ort to tell me I'd best leave Patience Appleby be! I don't mean to leave her be. I mean to let her know she can't ac' scandalous, and then set herself up as being as good's church folks and Christians. *I'll* give her her come-uppings!"

For probably the first time in his married life

Mr. Willis yielded to his feelings. "God-a'mighty, mother," he said; "sometimes you don't seem to have common sense! I reckon you'd best leave Patience Appleby be, if you know when you're well off." Then, frightened at what he had said, he walked on, hurriedly, swinging the lantern harder than ever.

Mrs. Willis walked behind him, dumb.

The day was cold and gray. Mrs. Willis opened with difficulty the broken-down gate that shut in Patience Appleby's house. "And no wonder," she thought, "it swags down so!"

There was a foot of snow on the ground. The path to the old, shabby house was trackless. Not a soul had been there since the snow fell—and that was two days ago! Mrs. Willis shivered under her warm shawl.

Patience opened the door. Her slow, heavy steps on the bare floor of the long hall affected Mrs. Willis strangely.

Patience was very tall and thin. She stooped, and her chest was sunken. She wore a dingy gray dress, mended in many places. There was a small, checked shawl folded in a "three-cornered" way about her shoulders. She coughed before she could greet her visitor.

" How d'you do, Mis' Willis," she said, at last.
" Come in, won't you? "

" How are you, Patience? " Mrs. Willis said,
and, to her own amazement, her voice did not
sound as stern as she had intended it should.

She had been practicing as she came along,
and this voice bore no resemblance whatever to
the one she had been having in her mind. Nor,
as she preceded Patience down the bare, draughty
hall to the sitting-room, did she bear herself with
that degree of frigid dignity which she had always considered most fitting to her position, both
socially and morally.

Somehow, the evidences of poverty on every
side chilled her blood. The sitting-room was
worse, even, than the hall. A big, empty room
with a small fire-place in one corner, wherein a
few coals were turning gray; a threadbare carpet, a couple of chairs, a little table with the
Bible on it, ragged wall-paper, and a shelf in one
corner filled with liniment bottles.

Mrs. Willis sat down in one of the rickety
chairs, and Patience, after stirring up the coals,
drew the other to the hearth.

" I'm afraid the room feels kind o' coolish," she
said. " I've got the last o' the coal on."

" D'you mean," said Mrs. Willis — and again
her voice surprised her — " that you're all out o'
coal? "

"All out." She drew the tiny shawl closer to her throat with trembling, bony fingers. "But Mis' Abernathy said she'd send me a scuttleful over today. I hate to take it from her, too ; her husband's lost his position and they ain't overly well off. But sence my rheumatiz has been so bad I can't earn a thing."

Mrs. Willis stared hard at the coals. For the life of her she could think of nothing but her own basement filled to the ceiling with coal.

"I reckon," said Patience, "you've come to hear my confessing-up?"

"Why — yes." Mrs. Willis started guiltily.

"What's the charges agen me, Mis' Willis?"

Mrs. Willis's eyelids fell heavily.

"Why, I reckon you know, Patience. You done wrong onct when you was a girl, and I don't think we'd ort to take you into the church tell you own up to it."

There was a little silence. Then Patience said, drawing her breath in heavily —"Mebbe I did do wrong onct when I was a little girl — only fourteen, say. But that's thirty year ago, and that's a long time, Mis' Willis. I don't think I'd ort to own up to it."

"*I* think you'd ort."

"Mis' Willis," — Patience spoke solemnly. "D'you think I'd ort to own up if it 'u'd affec' somebody else thet ain't never b'en talked about ?"

"Yes, I do," said Mrs. Willis, firmly. "If they deserve to be talked about, they'd *ort* to be talked about."

"Even if it was about the best folks in town?"

"Yes." Mrs. Willis thought of the minister.

"Even if it was about the best-off folks? Folks that hold their head the highest, and give most to churches and missionary; and thet ev'rybody looks up to?"

"Ye-es," said Mrs. Willis. That did not describe the minister, certainly. She could not have told you why her heart began to beat so violently. Somehow, she had been surprised out of the attitude she had meant to assume. Instead of walking in boldly and haughtily, and giving Patience her "come-uppings," she was finding it difficult to conquer a feeling of pity for the enemy because she was so poor and so cold. She must harden her heart.

"Even"—Patience lowered her eyes to the worn carpet—"if it was folks thet had b'en loudest condemin' other folks's sins, and that had bragged high and low thet there wa'n't no disgrace in their fambly, and never had b'en none, and who'd just be about killed by my confessing-up?"

"Yes," said Mrs. Willis, sternly. But she paled to the lips.

"I don't think so," said Patience, slowly. "I

234

think a body'd ort to have a chance if they want
to live better, without havin' anybody a-pryin'
into their effairs exceptin' God. But if you don't
agree with me, I'm ready to confess-up all *I've*
done bad. I guess you recollect, Mis' Willis,
thet your 'Lizy and me was just of an age, to a
day?"

Mrs. Willis's lips moved, but the words stuck
in her throat.

"And how we ust to play together and stay
nights with each other. We *loved* each other,
Mis' Willis. You ust to give us big slices o'
salt-risin' bread, spread thick with cream and
sprinkled with brown sugar — I can just see you
now, a-goin' out to the spring-house to get the
cream. And I can just taste it, too, when I get
good and hungry."

"What's all this got to do with your a-owning
up?" demanded Mrs. Willis, fiercely. "What's
my 'Lizy got to do with your going away that
time? Where was you at, Patience Appleby?"

"I'm comin' to that," said Patience, calmly;
but a deep flush came upon her face. "I've at-
toned-up fer that time, if any mortal bein' ever
did, Mis' Willis. I've had a hard life, but I've
never complained, because I thought the Lord
was a-punishin' me. But I have suffered. . . .
Thirty year, Mis' Willis, of prayin' to be fergive
fer one sin! But I ain't ever see the day I could

confess-up to 't — and I couldn't now, except to
'Lizy's mother."

An awful trembling shook Mrs. Willis's heart.
She looked at Patience with straining eyes. "Go
on," she said, hoarsely.

"'Lizy and me was fourteen on the same day.
She was goin' to Four Corners to visit her a'nt,
but I had to stay at home and work. I was
cryin' about it when, all of a sudden, 'Lizy
says — "Patience, let's up and have a good time
on our birthday !"

"Well, let's," I says, "but how?"

"I'll start fer Four Corners and then you run
away, and I'll meet you, and we'll go to Spring-
ville to the circus and learn to ride bareback"—

Mrs. Willis leaned forward in her chair. Her
face was very white ; her thin hands were clenched
so hard the knuckles stood out half an inch.

"Patience Appleby," she said, "you're a
wicked, sinful liar ! May the Lord A'mighty fergive you — *I* won't."

"I ain't askin' you to take my word ; you can
ask Mr. Willis hisself. He didn't go to Spring-
ville to buy him a horse, like he told you he did.
'Lizy and me had been at the circus two days
when she tuk sick, and I sent fer Mr. Willis un-
beknownst to anybody. He come and tuk her
home and fixed it all up with her a'nt at Four
Corners, and give out thet she'd been a-visitin'

there. But I had to sneak home alone and live
an outcast's life ever sence, and see her set up
above me — just because Mr. Willis got down to
beg me on his knees never to tell she was with
me. And I never did tell a soul, Mis' Willis, tell
last winter I was sick with a fever and told Mis'
Wincoop when I was out o' my head. But she's
never told anybody, either, and neither of us ever
will. Mr. Willis has helped me as much as he
could without your a-findin' it out, but I know how
it feels to be hungry and cold, and I know how it
feels to see Lizy set up over me, and marry rich,
and have nice children; and ride by me 'n her
kerriage without so much as lookin' at me — and
me a-chokin' with the dust off o' her kerriage
wheels. But I never complained none, and I ain't
a-complainin' now, Mis' Willis; puttin' 'Lizy
down wouldn't help me any. But I do think it's
hard if I can't be let into the church."

Her thin voice died away and there was silence.
Patience sat staring at the coals with the dullness
of despair on her face. Mrs. Willis's spare frame
had suddenly taken on an old, pathetic stoop.
What her haughty soul had suffered during that
recital, for which she had been so totally unpre-
pared, Patience would never realize. The world
seemed to be slipping from under the old woman's
trembling feet. She had been so strong in her
condemnation of sinners because she had felt so

sure she should never have any trading with sin herself. And lo ! all these years her own daughter — her one beloved child, dearer than life itself — had been as guilty as this poor outcast from whom she had always drawn her skirts aside, as from a leper. Ay, her daughter had been the guiltier of the two. She was not spared that bitterness, even. Her harsh sense of justice forced her to acknowledge, even in that first hour, that this woman had borne herself nobly, while her daughter had been a despicable coward.

It had been an erect, middle-aged woman who had come to give Patience Appleby her "come-uppings;" it was an old, broken-spirited one who went stumbling home in the early, cold twilight of the winter day. The fierce splendor of the sunset had blazed itself out; the world was a monotone in milky blue — save for one high line of dull crimson clouds strung along the horizon.

A shower of snow-birds sunk in Mrs. Willis's path, but she did not see them. She went up the path and entered her comfortable home ; and she fell down upon her stiff knees beside the first chair she came to — and prayed as she had never prayed before in all her hard and selfish life.

When Mr. Willis came home to supper he found his wife setting the table as usual. He started for the bedroom, but she stopped him.

"We're a-going to use the front bedroom after this, father," she said.

"Why, what are we going to do that fer, mother?"

"I'm a-going to give our'n to Patience Appleby."

"You're a-going to — *what*, mother?"

"I'm a-going to give our'n to Patience Appleby, I say. I'm a-going to bring her here to live, and she's got to have the warmest room in the house, because her rheumatiz is worse 'n mine. I'm a-going after her myself to-morrow in the kerriage." She turned and faced her husband sternly. "She's confessed-up ev'rything. I was dead set she should, and she has. I know where she was at, that time, and I know who was with her. I reckon I'd best be attoning up as well as Patience Appleby; and I'm going to begin by making her comf'terble and taking her into the church."

"Why, mother," said the old man, weakly. His wife repressed him with one look.

"Now, don't go to talking back, father," she said, sternly. "I reckon you kep' it from me fer the best, but it's turrable hard on me now. You get and wash yourself. I want that you should hold this candle while I fry the apple-fritters."

THE MOTHER OF "PILLS"

THE MOTHER OF "PILLS"

"Pills!   Oh, Pills!   You Pillsy!"

The girl turned from the door of the drug-store, and looked back under bent brows at her mother, who was wiping graduated glasses with a stained towel, at the end of the prescription counter.

"I wish you wouldn't call me that," she said; her tone was impatient but not disrespectful.

Her mother laughed. She was a big, good-natured looking woman, with light-blue eyes and sandy eyebrows and hair. She wore a black dress that had a cheap, white cord-ruche at the neck. There were spots down the front of her dress where acids had been spilled and had taken out the color.

"How particular we are gettin'," she said, turning the measuring glass round and round on the towel which had been wadded into it. "You didn't use to mind if I called you 'Pills,' just for fun."

"Well, I mind now."

The girl took a clean towel from a cupboard and began to polish the show-cases, breathing upon them now and then. She was a good-looking girl. She had strong, handsome features, and heavy brown hair, which she wore in a long braid down her back. A deep red rose was tucked in the girdle óf her cotton gown and its head lolled to and fro as she worked. Her hands were not prettily shaped, but sensitive, and the ends of the fingers were square.

"Well, Mariella, then," said Mrs. Mansfield, still looking amused; "I was goin' to ask you if you knew the Indians had all come in on their way home from hop pickin'."

Mariella straightened up and looked at her mother.

"Have they, honest, ma?"

"Yes, they have; they're all camped down on the beach."

"Oh, I wonder where!"

"Why, the Nooksacks are clear down at the coal-bunkers, an' the Lummies close to Timberline's Row; an' the Alaskas are all on the other side of the viaduct"

"Are they goin' to have the canoe race?"

"Yes, I guess so. I guess it'll be about sundown to-night. There, you forgot to dust that milk-shake. An' you ain't touched that shelf o' patent medicines!"

She set down the last graduate and hung the damp towel on a nail. Then she came out into the main part of the store and sat down comfortably behind the counter.

Long before Mariella was born her father had opened a drug-store in the tiny town of Sehome, on Puget Sound. There was a coal mine under the town. A tunnel led down into it, and the men working among the black diamonds, with their families, made up the town. But there was some trouble, and the mine was abandoned and flooded with salt water. The men went away, and for many years Sehome was little more than a name. A mail boat wheezed up from Seattle once a week; and two or three storekeepers — Mr. Mansfield among them — clung to the ragged edge of hope and waited for the boom. Before it came, Mr. Mansfield was bumped over the terrible road to the graveyard and laid down among the stones and ferns. Then Mrs. Mansfield "run" the store. The question "Can you fill perscriptions?" was often put to her fearfully by timid customers, but she was equal to the occasion.

"Well, I guess I can," she would say, squaring about and looking her questioner unwaveringly in the eye. "I guess I'd ought to. I've been in the store with my husband, that's dead, for twenty years. I'm not a regular, but I'm a practical — an' that's better than a regular any day."

"It's not so much what you know in a drug-store as what you *look* like you know," she some-times confided to admiring friends.

It is true Mrs. Mansfied was often perplexed over the peculiar curdled appearance of some mixture — being as untaught in the mysterious ways of emulsions as a babe — but such trifles were dismissed with a philosophical sigh, and the prescriptions were handed over the counter with a complaisance that commanded confidence. The doctor hinted, with extreme delicacy, at times, that his emulsions did not turn out as smooth as he had expected ; or that it would be agreeable to find some of his aqueous mixtures tinged with cochineal ; or that it was possible to make pills in such a way that they would not — so to speak — melt in the patient's mouth before he could swallow them. But Mrs. Mansfield invari-ably laughed at him in a kind of motherly way, and reminded him that he ought to be glad to have even a "practical" in a place like Sehome. And really this was so true that it was unanswer-able.

So Mrs. Mansfield held the fort ; and as her medicines, although abominable to swallow, never killed any one, she was looked upon with awe and respect by the villagers and the men in the neighboring logging-camps.

Mariella was brought up in the drug-store. She had the benefit of her mother's experience, and, besides that, she had studied the "dispensatory"—a word, by the way, which Mrs. Mansfield began with a capital letter because of the many pitfalls from which it had rescued her.

"Mariella is such a good girl," her mother frequently declared; "she got a real good education over at the Whatcom schools, an' she's such a help in the drug-store. She does make a beautiful pill."

Indeed, the girl's pill-making accomplishment was so appreciated by Mrs. Mansfield that she had nick-named her "Pills"—a name that had been the cause of much mirth between them.

Mariella was now sixteen, and the long-deferred "boom" was upon them. Mrs. Mansfield and her daughter contemplated it from the store door daily with increasing admiration. The wild clover no longer velveted the middle of the street. New buildings, with red, green or blue fronts and non-descript backs, leaped up on every corner and in between corners. The hammers and saws made music sweeter than any brass band to Sehome ears. Day and night the forests blazed backward from the town. When there were no customers in the store Mariella stood in the door, twisting the rope of the awning around her wrist, and watched the flames leaping from limb to limb up the tall, straight fir-trees. When Sehome hill was burning at night, it was a magnificent spectacle; like hundreds of torches dipped into a very hell of fire and lifted to heaven by invisible hands —while in the East the noble, white dome of Mount Baker burst out of the darkness against the lurid sky. The old steamer *Idaho* came down from Seattle three times a week now. When she landed, Mrs. Mansfield and Mariella, and such customers as chanced to be in the store, hurried breathlessly back to the little sitting-room, which overlooked the bay, to count the passengers. The old colony wharf, running a mile out across the tide-lands to deep water, would be "fairly alive with 'em," Mrs. Mansfield declared daily, in an ecstasy of anticipation of the good times their coming foretold. She counted never less than a hundred and fifty; and so many walked three and four abreast that it was not possible to count all.

Really, that summer everything seemed to be going Mrs. Mansfield's way. Mariella was a comfort to her mother and an attraction to the store; business was excellent; her property was worth five times more than it had ever been before; and, besides — when her thoughts reached this point Mrs. Mansfield smiled consciously and blushed — there was Mr. Grover! Mr. Grover kept the dry-goods store next door. He had come at the very beginning of the boom. He was slim and dark and forty. Mrs. Mansfield was forty and large and fair. Both were "well off." Mr. Grover was lonely and "dropped into" Mrs. Mansfield's little sitting-room every night. She invited him to supper frequently, and he told her her that her fried chicken and "cream" potatoes were better than anything he had eaten since his mother died. Of late his intentions were not to be misunderstood, and Mrs. Mansfield was already putting by a cozy sum for a wedding outfit. Only that morning she had looked at herself in the glass more attentively than usual while combing her hair. Some thought made her blush and smile.

"You ought to be ashamed!" she said, shaking her head at herself in the glass as at a gay, young thing. "To be thinkin' about gettin' married! With a big girl like Pills too. One good thing: He really seems to think as much of Pills as you do yourself, Mrs. Mansfield. That's what makes me so — happy, I guess. I believe it's the first time I ever was real happy before." She sighed unconsciously as she glanced back over her years of married life. "An' I don't know what makes me so awful happy now. But sometimes when I get up of a mornin' I just feel

as if I could go out on the hill an' sing — foolish
as any of them larks holler'n' for joy.

"Mariella," she said, watching the duster in
the girl's hands, "what made you flare up so
when I called you 'Pills?' You never done that
before, an' I don't see what ails you all of a sudden."

"I didn't mean to flare up," said Mariella.
She opened the cigar-case and arranged the boxes
carefully. Then she closed it with a snap and
looked at her mother. "But I wish you'd stop
it, ma. Mr. Grover said——"

"Well, what 'id he say?"

"He said it wasn't a nice name to call a girl
by." Mariella's face reddened, but she was stooping behind the counter.

Mrs. Mansfield drummed on the show-case with
broad fingers and looked thoughtful.

"Well," she said with significance, after a
pause, "if he don't like it, I won't do it. We've
had lots o' fun over it, Pills, ain't we — I mean
Mariella — but I guess he has a right to say what
you'll be called, Pi—— my dear."

"Oh, ma," said Mariella. Her face was like
a poppy.

"Well, I guess you won't object, will you?
I've been wond'rin' how you felt about it."

"Oh, ma," faltered the girl; "do you think,
honest, he——he——"

"Yes, I do," replied her mother, laughing comfortably and blushing faintly. "I'm sure of it. An' I'm happier 'n I ever was in my life over it. I don't think I could give you a better stepfather, or one that would think more of you."

Mariella stood up slowly behind the counter and looked — stared — across the room at her mother, in a dazed, uncomprehending way. The color ebbed slowly out of her face. She did not speak, but she felt the muscles about her mouth jerking. She pressed her lips more tightly together.

"I hope you don't think I oughtn't to marry again," said her mother, returning her look without understanding it in the least. "Your pa's been dead ten years"— this in an injured tone. "There ain't many women —— Oh, good mornin', Mr. Lester? Mariella, 'll you wait on Mr. Lester? Well"— beaming good naturedly on her customer —"how's real estate this mornin'? Any new sales afoot?"

"*Are* there?" repeated that gentleman, leaning on the show-case and lighting his cigar, innocent of intentional discourtesy. "Well, I should *smile* —and smile broadly too, Mrs. Mansfield. There's a Minneapolis chap here that's buyin' right an' left ; just *slashin*' things ! He's bought a lot o' water-front property, too ; an' let me tell *you*, right now, that Jim Hill's behind him ; an'

251

Jim Hill's the biggest railroad man in the U. S. to-day, an' the Great Northern's behind *him !*"

"Well, I hope so." Mrs. Mansfield drew a long breath of delight. Mr. Lester smiled, shrugged his shoulders, spread out his hands, and sauntered out with the air of a man who has the ear of railroad kings.

"Are you goin' to the canoe races to-night, Mariella?" began her mother, in a conciliatory tone.

"I don't know. Might as well, I guess."

The girl was wiping the shelf bottles now ; her face was pale, but her back was to her mother.

"Well, we will have an early supper, so you can get off. Mercy, child ! Did you break one o' them glass labels ? How often 'v' I told you not to press on 'em so hard ? What one is it ? The tincture cantharides ! Well, tie a string around it, so we'll know what it is. There ain't no label on the aconite bottle, nor the Jamaica ginger either — an' them settin' side by side, too. I hate guessin' at things in a drug-store — 'specially when one's a poison. Have you scoured up them spatulas ?"

"Yes'm."

"Well, I'll go in an' do up the dishes, an' leave you to 'tend store. Don't forget to make Mr. Benson's pills."

But Mr. Benson's pills were not made right

away. When her mother was gone, Mariella got down from the step-ladder and leaned one elbow on the show-case and rested her chin in her hand. Her throat swelled in and out fitfully, and the blue veins showed, large and full, on her temples. For a long time she stood thus, twisting the towel in her hand and looking at the fires on the hill without seeing them. Some of their dry burning seemed to get into her own eyes.

Mr. Grover, passing, glanced in.

"Mariella," he said, putting one foot across the threshold, "are you goin' to the canoe races?"

The girl had darted erect instantly, and put on a look of coquettish indifference.

"Yes, I am." Her eyes flashed at him over her shoulder from the corners of their lids as she started back to the prescription-case. "I'm goin' with Charlie Walton!"

When Mariella had gone to the races that night, and customers were few and far between, Mr. Grover walked with a determined air through Mrs. Mansfield's store and, pushing aside the crimson canton-flannel portieres, entered her cheerful sitting-room. On the floor was a Brussels carpet, large-flowered and vivid. A sewing-machine stood in one corner and Mariella's organ in another. The two narrow windows over-looking the sound were gay with blooming geraniums and white curtains tied with red ribbons. There was a trunk deceptively stuffed and cretonned into the semblance of a settee; and there was a wicker-chair that was full of rasping, aggravating noises when you rocked in it. It had red ribbon twisted through its back and arms. Mrs. Mansfield was sitting in it now, reading a novel, and the chair was complaining unceasingly.

Mr. Grover sat down on the trunk.

"Mrs. Mansfield," he said, looking squarely at her, "I've got somethin' to ask of you, an' I'm goin' to do it while Mariella's away."

"That so?" said Mrs. Mansfield.

The color in her cheek deepened almost to a purple. She put one hand up to her face, and with the other nervously wrinkled the corners of the leaves of her novel. She lowered her lids resolutely to hide the sudden joy in her eyes.

"I guess you know what I've been comin' here so much for. I couldn't help thinkin', too, that you liked the idea an' was sort of encouragin' me."

Mrs. Mansfield threw one hand out toward him in a gesture at once deprecating, coquettish and helpful.

"Oh, you!" she exclaimed, laughing and coloring more deeply. There was decided encouragement in her honest blue eyes under their sandy lashes.

254

"Well, didn't you, now?" Mr. Grover leaned toward her.

She hesitated, fingering the leaves of her book. She turned her head to one side; the leaves swished softly as they swept past her broad thumb; the corners of her mouth curled in a tremulous smile; the fingers of her other hand moved in an unconscious caress across her warm cheek; she remembered afterward that the band across the bay on the long pier, where the races were, was playing "Annie Laurie," and that the odor of wild musk, growing outside her window in a box, was borne in, sweet and heavy, by the sea winds. It was the one perfect moment of Mrs. Mansfield's life — in which there had been no moments that even approached perfection; in which there had been no hint of poetry — only dullest, everyday prose. She had married because she had been taught that women should marry; and Mr. Mansfield had been a good husband. She always said that; and she did not even know that she always sighed after saying it. Her regard for Mr. Grover was the poetry — the wine — of her hard, frontier life. Never before that summer had she stood and listened to the message of the meadow-lark with a feeling of exaltation that brought tears to her eyes; or gone out to gather wild pink clover with the dew on it; or turned her broad foot aside to spare a worm.

Not that Mr. Grover ever did any of these things ; but that love had lifted the woman's soul and given her the new gift of seeing the beauty of common things. No one had guessed that there was a change in her heart, not even Mariella.

It was well that Mrs. Mansfield prolonged that perfect moment. When she did lift her eyes there was a kind of appealing tenderness in them.

"I guess I did," she said.

"Well, then,"— Mr. Grover drew a breath of relief —"you might's well say I can have her. I want it all understood before she gets home. I want to stop her runnin' with that Walton. Once or twice I've been afraid you'd just as leave she'd marry him as me. I don't like to see girls gallivant with two or three fellows."

Mrs. Mansfield sat motionless, looking at him. Her eyes did not falter ; the smile did not wholly vanish from her face. Only the blood throbbed slowly away, leaving it paler than Mariella's had been that morning. She understood her mistake almost before his first sentence. While he was speaking her thoughts were busy. She felt the blood coming back when she remembered what she had said to Mariella. If *only* she had not spoken !

"Well," she said, calmly, "have you said anything to Mariella ?"

"Yes, I have ; lots o' times. An' I know she

likes me ; but she's some flirtish, and that's what
I want to put a stop to. So, with your permis-
sion, I'll have a talk with her to-night.''

"I'd like to talk to her first myself.'' Mrs.
Mansfield looked almost stern. "But I guess
it'll be all right, Mr. Grover. If you'd just as
soon wait till to-morrow, I'd like to be alone and
make up my mind what to say to her.''

Mr. Grover got up and shook hands with her
awkwardly.

"I'll make her a good husband,'' he said, earnestly.

"I don't doubt that,'' replied Mrs. Mansfield.
Then he went out and the crimson curtain fell
behind him.

When Mariella came home her mother was sitting, rocking, by the window. The lamp was
lighted.

"Pills,'' she said, "I want you to stop goin'
with that fello'.''

The girl looked at her in silence. Then she
took off her turban and stuck the long black pins
back into it.

"I thought you liked him,'' she said, slowly.

"I do, but Mr. Grover wants you — an' I like
him better.''

"Wants *me !*'' Mariella drew up her shoulders proudly. 257

"Yes, you," replied Mrs. Mansfield, laughing. The humor of the situation was beginning to appeal to her. " He says he'd told you. You must of laughed after I told you he wanted me."

" Oh, ma, does he want me, honest ?"

" Yes, he does." She was still laughing.

" An' don't you mind, ma ?"

" Not a mite," said the widow, cheerfully. " I'd rather he'd marry you than me ; only, I thought he was too nice a man to be lost to the fam'ly."

" Oh, ma !"

" Well, get to bed now. He's comin' in the mornin' to see you."

She took up the lamp and stood holding it irresolutely.

" Pills," she said, looking embarrassed, " You won't ever tell him that I —— that I——"

" Never, ma !" exclaimed the girl, earnestly ; " as long as I live."

" All right, then. Look out ! You're droppin' tallo' from your candle ! Don't hold it so crooked, child ! I wouldn't like him to laugh about it. Good-night."

As she passed through the kitchen she called out : " Oh, Pills ! Mr. Jordan brought in a mess of trout. We'll have 'em fried for breakfast."

The girl came running after her mother, and threw her arms around her.

"Oh, ma, are you sure you don't care a bit?"

"Not a bit," said Mrs. Mansfield, kissing her heartily. "I just thought he ought to be in the family. I'm glad it's turned out this way. Now, you go to bed, an' don't forget to roll up your bangs."

She went into her room and shut the door.

MRS. RISLEY'S CHRISTMAS DINNER

MRS. RISLEY'S CHRISTMAS DINNER

She was an old, old woman. She was crippled with rheumatism and bent with toil. Her hair was gray,—not that lovely white that softens and beautifies the face, but harsh, grizzled gray. Her shoulders were round, her chest was sunken, her face had many deep wrinkles. Her feet were large and knotty ; her hands were large, too, with great hollows running down their backs. And how painfully the cords stood out in her old, withered neck !

For the twentieth time she limped to the window and flattened her face against the pane. It was Christmas day. A violet sky sparkled coldly over the frozen village. The ground was covered with snow ; the roofs were white with it. The chimneys looked redder than usual as they emerged from its pure drifts and sent slender curls of electric-blue smoke into the air.

The wind was rising. Now and then it came sweeping down the hill, pushing a great sheet of snow, powdered like dust, before it. The window-sashes did not fit tightly, and some of it sifted into the room and climbed into little cones on the floor. Snow-birds drifted past, like soft, dark shadows ; and high overhead wild geese went sculling through the yellow air, their mournful "hawnk-e-hawnk-hawnks" sinking downward like human cries.

As the old woman stood with her face against the window and her weak eyes strained down the street, a neighbor came to the door.

"Has your daughter an' her fambly come yet, Mis' Risley?" she asked, entering sociably.

"Not yet," replied Mrs. Risley, with a good attempt at cheerfulness; but her knees suddenly began shaking, and she sat down.

"Why, she'd ought to 'a' come on the last train, hadn't she?"

"Oh, I do' know. There's a plenty o' time. Dinner won't be ready tell two past."

"She ain't b'en to see you fer five year, has she?" said the neighbor. "I reckon you'll have a right scrumptious set-out fer 'em?"

"I will so," said Mrs. Risley, ignoring the other question. "Her husband's comin'."

"I want to know! Why, he just thinks he's some punkins, I hear."

"Well, he's rich enough to think hisself anything he wants to." Mrs. Risley's voice took on a tone of pride.

"I sh'u'd think you'd want to go an' live with 'em. It's offul hard fer you to live here all alone, with your rheumatiz."

Mrs. Risley stooped to lay a stick of wood on the fire.

"I've worked nigh onto two weeks over this dinner," she said, "a-seed'n' raisins an' cur'nts, an' things. I've hed to skimp harrable, Mis' Tomlinson, to get it; but it's just—*perfec'*. Roast goose an' cranberry sass, an' cel'ry soup, an' mince an' punkin pie,—to say nothin' o' plum-puddin'! An' cookies an' cur'nt-jell tarts fer the children. I'll hev to wear my old under-clo's all winter to pay fer 't; but I don't care."

"I sh'u'd think your daughter'd keep you more comf'terble, seein' her husband's so rich."

There was a silence. Mrs. Risley's face grew stern. The gold-colored cat came and arched her back for a caress. "My bread riz beautiful," Mrs. Risley said then. "I worried so over 't. An' my fruit-cake smells that good when I open the stun crock! I put a hull cup o' brandy in it. Well, I guess you'll hev to excuse me. I've got to set the table."

When Mrs. Tomlinson was gone, the strained look came back to the old woman's eyes. She went on setting the table, but at the sound of a wheel, or a step even, she began to tremble and put her hand behind her ear to listen.

"It's funny they *didn't* come on that last train," she said. "I w'u'dn't tell her, though. But they'd ort to be here by this time."

She opened the oven door. The hot, delicious odor of its precious contents gushed out. Did ever goose brown so perfectly before? And how large the liver was! It lay in the gravy in one corner of the big dripping-pan, just beginning to curl at the edges. She tested it carefully with a little three-tined iron fork.

The mince-pie was on the table, waiting to be warmed, and the pumpkin-pie was out on the back porch,—from which the cat had been excluded for the present. The cranberry sauce, the celery in its high, old-fashioned glass, the little bee-hive of hard sauce for the pudding and the thick cream for the coffee, bore the pumpkin-pie company. The currant jelly in the tarts glowed like great red rubies set in circles of old gold; the mashed potatoes were light and white as foam.

For one moment, as she stood there in the savory kitchen, she thought of the thin, worn flannels, and how much better her rheumatism would be with the warm ones which could have been bought with the money spent for this dinner. Then she flushed with self-shame.

"I must be gittin' childish," she exclaimed, indignantly; "to begredge a Chris'mas dinner to 'Lizy. 'S if I hedn't put up with old underclo's afore now! But I will say there ain't many women o' my age thet c'u'd git up a dinner like this 'n',—rheumatiz an' all."

A long, shrill whistle announced the last train

from the city. Mrs. Risley started and turned pale. A violent trembling seized her. She could scarcely get to the window, she stumbled so. On the way she stopped at the old walnut bureau to put a lace cap on her white hair and to look anxiously into the mirror.

"Five year!" she whispered. "It's an offul spell to go without seein' your only daughter! Everything'll seem mighty poor an' shabby to her, I reckon,— her old mother worst o' all. I never sensed how I'd changed tell now. My! how no-account I'm a gittin'! I'm all of a trimble!"

Then she stumbled on to the window and pressed her cheek against the pane.

"They'd ort to be in sight now," she said. But the minutes went by, and they did not come.

"Mebbe they've stopped to talk, meetin' folks," she said, again. "But they'd ort to be in sight now." She trembled so she had to get a chair and sit down. But still she wrinkled her cheek upon the cold pane and strained her dim eyes down the street.

After a while a boy came whistling down from the corner. There was a letter in his hand. He stopped and rapped, and when she opened the door with a kind of frightened haste, he gave her the letter and went away, whistling again.

A letter! Why should a letter come? Her heart was beating in her throat now,— that poor old heart that had beaten under so many sorrows ! She searched in a dazed way for her glasses. Then she fell helplessly into a chair and read it :

"DEAR MOTHER,—I am so sorry we cannot come, after all. We just got word that Robert's aunt has been expecting us all the time, because we've spent every Christmas there. We feel as if we *must* go there, because she always goes to so much trouble to get up a fine dinner ; and we knew you wouldn't do that. Besides, she is so rich ; and one has to think of one's children, you know. We'll come, *sure*, next year. With a merry, merry Christmas from all,   ELIZA."

It was hard work reading it, she had to spell out so many of the words. After she had finished, she sat for a long, long time motionless, looking at the letter. Finally the cat came and rubbed against her, "myowing" for her dinner. Then she saw that the fire had burned down to a gray, desolate ash.

She no longer trembled, although the room was cold. The wind was blowing steadily now. It was snowing, too. The bleak Christmas afternoon and the long Christmas night stretched before her. Her eyes rested upon the little fir-tree on a table in one corner, with its gilt balls and strings of popcorn and colored candles. She could not bear the sight of it. She got up stiffly.

"Well, kitten," she said, trying to speak cheerfully, but with a pitiful break in her voice, "let's go out an' eat our Christmas dinner."

268